Fiery Bride

CYNTHIA WOOLF

DEDICATION

For Jim. My best friend, my lover, my husband. Without your support none of this would be possible. I love you more than words can ever express.

CONTENTS

ACKNOWLEDGMENTS

To my critique partners, Karen Docter, Michele Callahan, Jennifer Zane and Kally Jo Surbeck, thank you for your help and critiques and Just Write sessions so I could get this done. Thanks for helping me when writers block hit, I couldn't get through it without each of you.

To my editor, Kally Jo Surbeck, thank you for your unwavering support and advice. You make my life so much easier.

CHAPTER 1

April 30, 1871

"What do you mean, you quit? Mr. Sinclair, you just can't quit." Margaret "Maggie" Selby put her pen down on the desk. She would not raise her voice. She would not lose control.

"I'm sorry, Mrs. Selby, but I got no choice. There's an opening at the sanitarium in Albany and my Mary, she needs to go right now. The doctors there might be able to help her. We leave on the morning train."

Maggie took a deep breath and nodded. She understood. She really did, but it didn't change the fact that she was now in a difficult situation. "Of course, you must go. I know how poor Mary's health is and any help that can be obtained for her, must be."

"I wish I could give you some notice, but we just received the letter in yesterday's post."

"It's fine, Mr. Sinclair. I'll manage."

He handed her an envelope. "Here are the train tickets."

"Yes, well, I've wanted to see the frontier I've been sending my girls to. I'm simply going to see it sooner than I anticipated."

"I'm truly sorry, Mrs. Selby."

Maggie got up, came around the desk and held her hand out to him. "You just take care of Mary. That's your job now."

He shook her hand, nodded. Mr. Sinclair put on his hat and wiped his brow with his kerchief before venturing back out into the already hot and sunny morning.

She went to her desk, grabbed Caleb Black's file, put the closed sign on the door and then went upstairs to her apartment to pack. Her bride, Jenny Talbot would be by in an hour or so to pick up her tickets. Maggie would tell her then that she'd be accompanying her, not Mr. Sinclair. It was just as well. Jenny was nervous as a kitten and Maggie worried about the union, but both Mr. Black and Jenny had been adamant that it take place. If truth be told, Maggie herself was a better match for Mr. Black than Jenny. But she was here to find matches for others, not for herself.

Jenny's reasoning she understood. Jenny was the oldest of the seven Talbot children. At twenty-two years old, felt she was a burden on her parents even though she worked and helped out with the bills. She hated her job and wanted to get married. Her chances were growing slim. Most men of marriageable age were either already married, old or widowers with hellions for children.

Jenny was a tall, slim girl with pale blue eyes and dark blond hair. Her lips were full, her nose long and straight. Just a plain young woman from a struggling family who wanted a better life. One that the wild frontier might be able to offer.

Mr. Black's reasoning was less clear. He was successful and wanted children. Maggie had presented him with several other possible candidates, some more attractive, some younger, some older, all of whom he'd rejected. The reasons he gave were weak. Brown hair. Too short. Too fat. Too thin. Too young. Too old. There seemed to be a reason for rejecting every one she sent him.

Finally, he'd settled on Jenny with the proviso that Maggie herself accompanied the girl. She'd agreed, but stated only that Jenny would be accompanied. With her full intention having been to send Mr. Sinclair in her place. Maggie's time was much more well spent here in New York. Finding clients, assigning candidates that is where her mind, body and commitment lay. Yes, running her business is where she belonged, more than on a trip to the wild West. She didn't feel bad about her decision. Really she didn't, she told herself over and over. But she was lying. If she were honest, deep down she was afraid to meet Mr. Black.

Afraid her image of him would be wrong, but even more afraid it would be right and he really was the man he depicted in his letters.

She shouldn't have allowed it, the private correspondence, but it had been innocent enough. In the beginning. A simple flirtation with someone she'd never meet. But now, the thought of actually meeting him terrified and thrilled her at the same time. Now she had to go. Maggie released a rather breathless sigh. She blinked repeatedly against the harsh sunlight. So Mr. Black was getting what he'd asked for after all. Much to her dismay.

The building she lived in was one of her late husband Edgar's rental properties, but after having to sell everything else, it was all that was left. She hadn't lived in the small apartment with her husband and she was glad of that. The fewer memories of Edgar, the better. She'd gotten rid of most everything they'd had. She'd even sold their china and bought a cheaper, but prettier replacement. There were, of course, some things she kept, such as her clothes and jewelry. She'd sold only the ugliest pieces of jewelry and only as she'd needed in order to survive. That was before her business took off. It had taken five long years to get where she was today. And the worst of those days was better than any with Edgar. She was free of him. Forever. Never again would a man touch her in anger. Never would another man hit her.

She was even starting to think that maybe it was time to contemplate another relationship. Not a marriage, but a companion. Someone she could talk to, go to dinner with, perhaps even love. *If* she did find a person to share her life with, it would be on her terms. This time she would make her own decision, not endure her father's wishes. She would never settle for another Edgar. There had to be good men out there. Caleb Black seemed to be one. But who could tell from a letter, or even a dozen letters? Still, when she thought of him, her stomach did a little flip and her heart beat a little faster, all of which only made her more wary. But he was hundreds of miles away. And in New York, well…things were different. She had no social life.

No place to find someone. That's what she told herself. Repeatedly.

Taking her two valises out from under the bed, she packed them each with two full changes of clothing and some necessary sundries, such as her toothbrush and tooth powder, hairbrush and extra hairpins. She'd long ago given up wearing corsets. She had no one to help her into and out of one, so there wasn't much point in buying them. Besides, she had a good figure and didn't need the corset, especially in this heat. Just a chemise would do. She was a little plump, but that only gave her lush curves.

Once she was packed, she sat down to read the file again like she'd done dozens of times before. She was fascinated by Mr. Caleb Black. He was handsome. Not a dandy. Masculine. Strong. His photograph showed a square jaw and dark eyes. His hair was brown or black, she couldn't tell which, in the tin type he'd sent. His shoulders appeared wide and his waist trim. He wore a three piece suit with a tie and held a Stetson hat in his hand. She'd asked him in one of her letters what kind of hat it was, as she'd never seen any like it before. She'd asked him a lot of things in her letters and he wrote back quickly with the answers. Well, as quickly as the mail went, which was about two weeks. He asked her questions about her life. What she liked and didn't.

He included snippets of his life story with each letter. In reality, he'd said more about himself to her than he did in any of his letters to Jenny. Those were sterile. Formal. There was nothing of himself in them. Nothing of his sense of humor, his love for his daughter or his fierce protectiveness of her. All of him, everything that made him special, was in his letters to Maggie, not the ones to Jenny. And he insisted on calling her Maggie, no matter how many times she'd told him her name was Margaret. She kept trying to be mad, but it brought back better days. Days before Edgar and the mess that was their marriage.

And Maggie had read every letter he'd sent to Jenny. She read all the letters to her brides to make certain that what these men promised the young women they were to marry was even possible, much less true. She'd had one man promise a girl she'd be clothed in silk and showered in gold. Needless to say, since the man had to make installments to Maggie, she didn't pass on the letter and she'd sent the man back his money. She told him unequivocally that she helped only men who were truthful with her and her brides. Maggie had to protect the women and her business by making sure the men were trustworthy.

Now she'd meet Caleb Black. If she admitted it to herself, she was a little excited. Finally able to get acquainted with the man she'd secretly been dreaming about but couldn't have. No. Not without ruining Jenny's life. She would never do that. It was her business, her life, and she'd protect it at all costs.

*****

On the train Maggie watched Jenny and the young man from her seat near the window. She had it down because the heat in the train car was stifling. Even the smell of the coal burning was preferable to the unbearable temperature in the car. The wind blew through her hair and cooled her, a bit.

Robert Gordon was the man's name but Jenny called him Robbie. He was near to her age and she was definitely attracted. He had brown hair. Just an average looking man. Not quite six feet, he was still several inches taller than Jenny.

That they were infatuated with each other worried Maggie. She would have to remind Jenny of her obligation to Mr. Black. She was about to do just that when Jenny got up and walked toward her. The determined expression on her face didn't bode well for Maggie or, she was afraid, for Mr. Black.

"Maggie," began Jenny.

"I'm not sure I want to hear this," replied Maggie.

"I've accepted Robbie's marriage proposal. We're in love, Maggie, and I'd like your blessing but I'm going to do it whether you approve or not. Please Maggie, you're the closest person to a mother I've got."

She looked up into Jenny's blue eyes and saw the grim determination but she had to give it a try. "And what of Mr. Black? You've given him your agreement to marry him." Maggie knew it was hopeless as soon as Jenny mentioned love.

Jenny wrung her hands and sat in the seat opposite Maggie. "Don't you understand? Mr. Black is just a name and a picture. Robbie is real. I can touch him, talk to him and even kiss him if I want to. I feel what he feels. He's my Robbie."

"Jenny…,"

She got up and gazed back down at Maggie. "You can't change my mind and you can't stop me. Robbie lives in Omaha and we'll be getting off the train there. He's part owner in a hardware store. We'll go directly to the Justice of the Peace to see if he can marry us right away."

Maggie stood and placed her hand on Jenny's arm. "If this is the course you are determined to take, then you have my blessing. I wish you and Robbie all the happiness in the world."

"Thank you," whispered Jenny as though she'd been holding her breath waiting for Maggie's answer. She wrapped Maggie in her embrace. "Thank you so much."

"You're welcome. Just be happy."

"We will." She started to walk away, then stopped and turned back to Maggie. "What will you tell Mr. Black?"

"The truth."

*****

May 8, 1871

She'd done nothing but worry about it for the last two days and now that the train pulled to a stop in front of the depot in Denver, she was out of time. Maggie looked out the window and saw mountains standing tall in the distance. They appeared purple. Snow still covered the tallest peaks even now in the spring. They stood bright against a sky so blue it reminded her of her childhood on the farm in upstate New York, with its clear skies and starry nights. The soot in the New York City air kept the sky looking gray most of the time. She hadn't realized how much she missed it being so clear.

The beauty didn't escape her even if her nerves prevented her from fully enjoying it. She rose from her seat and smoothed her skirt preparing to meet Mr. Black. How she would tell him that she had arrived without his bride she didn't know. Taking a deep breath, she put her shoulders back and walked off the train.

Maggie removed her gloves and shook them. The ash and soot made a small dust cloud. It was hard to believe they still managed to appear mostly black despite the dirt. She neatly folded them and placed them in one of the valises at her feet. She stood on the platform in the late afternoon sun waiting for Mr. Black. Sweat trickled between her breasts and she wanted nothing more than to cleanse her body with a cold cloth and lie naked in a cool, dark room with a breeze from an open window flowing over her. Instead she watched as couples reunited with loving embraces. Families welcomed home fathers and brothers, sisters and mothers from trips to the east. The pang in her heart reminded her she had no one in her life that would miss her or welcome her home.

She was so caught up in the reunions she hadn't noticed the tall man's approach.

"Mrs. Selby?" asked a deep baritone voice from behind her.

She spun around and looked up, way up, into dark, coffee colored eyes. "Yes."

The man removed his worn leather gloves and held his hand out to her. "Caleb Black."

"Mr. Black," she said grasping his hand firmly. "I'm so...pleased to finally meet you." She stumbled over the words as his hand engulfed hers with warmth.

"As I am you, though I'm somewhat surprised. You made it fairly clear you wouldn't accompany Miss Talbot and that I was to meet her with Mr. Sinclair."

She dropped her gaze and realized their hands were still clasped and quickly extricated herself from his grasp. "Yes, well about that...,"

"I'm listening," he said quietly.

"Mr. Sinclair had a family emergency before he and Jenny were to leave, so I had to accompany her myself."

"That explains Mr. Sinclair's absence," he looked around them, "but not Miss Talbots. Is she still on the train?"

Maggie took a deep, steadying breath and braced herself. "Jenny met a man on the train and abandoned me in Omaha to marry him." She rushed on, "I'm so sorry Mr. Black. It'll take a little time but I'll refund your money as soon as I return to New York."

He cocked his head to one side and said, "I don't want a refund, Mrs. Selby. I want a wife."

"I don't have one for you, Mr. Black."

"Ah, but you do." He smiled and she swore his eyes twinkled with merriment. "You have *you*." He looked her up and down. "And I think you'll do just dandy."

Maggie stood there with her mouth agape until he reached over and gently lifted her chin with his knuckle.

"You can't be serious," she finally said. Guilty she'd been lusting after one of her clients. One of her bride's suitors.

"But I am. I think we'll suit."

"We most certainly will not suit." She almost stomped her foot in anger, but she wasn't really angry. She actually couldn't blame him. And getting angry wouldn't solve anything.

He smiled, tucked his thumbs in his belt and rocked back on his heels. Then he asked her, "What's waiting for you back in New York, Maggie?"

"Don't call me Maggie."

"Fine. What's waiting for you...*Margaret*? You have no husband, no family. I know you don't from your letters."

"I have a business."

He took her hands in his and began making small circles on the inside of her wrists with his thumbs. "A business can't warm your bed at night. A business can't hold you or laugh with you. Come with me. Have supper with me. Let's talk about it."

"I...I don't know."

"Wait just one minute there, young man. I've come to meet Mrs. Selby, too."

Maggie looked at the newcomer, shocked that anyone else would have known her name. He was an older man, in his sixties. About the same height as Maggie with gray hair and long gray beard.

"And you are?" asked Maggie.

"I'm Martin Butler and I've a bone to pick with you. My bride ran off and if you're going to take the place of a runaway bride, it's going to be mine." He grabbed her arm.

Maggie tried to shake him loose but he was strong.

Caleb had no problem stepping in. He took the man's wrist with his right hand and sent a left hook to Butler's jaw, sending him backwards to the ground. Butler released Maggie as he fell. His hand went immediately to his jaw.

"Do not touch Mrs. Selby." Caleb's voice was

soft, steely .

"Owww. Alright. Alright." He backed away, out of Caleb's reach.

Maggie moved closer to Caleb and peeked around his shoulder. "You're Mr. Butler? You're supposed to be forty years old. You're sixty-five if you're a day. No wonder Beatrice ran away. You lied to me and for some reason, Mr. Sinclair didn't tell me your real age. Why is that, I wonder? And how did you know I'd be here?"

Martin shrugged. "I telegraphed your office. Your girl, Sally, wired me back where'd you be. As to the man, Sinclair. Enough money in the right hands can do wonders as keeping someone's mouth shut."

Maggie sucked in a breath, "That's how he got the money for Mary's doctors." She couldn't really blame Mr. Sinclair. His wife, Mary, needed the treatments or she was going to die. If it was someone Maggie loved, she'd have done everything possible, as well. She looked over at Mr. Butler. His shaggy gray hair hanging lank around his collar and his long silver beard lying on his chest. His eyes sparkled with mischief or something more sinister, she wasn't sure. She was sure that if she'd been Beatrice she'd have bolted, too. "You lied on your application and therefore our contract is null and void. Now if you'll excuse me, I have an appointment with Mr. Black."

Maggie took Caleb's arm. "Shall we?"

Caleb scooped up both her bags in one hand, "We shall."

They'd walked about half way down the platform when she stopped and turned back. Martin Butler stood there watching them, hands clenched into fists. The look in his eyes along with the long hair and beard gave him a feral appearance and somewhat frightened Maggie. She was glad of Caleb's assistance.

"You can let go of me now."

"Not yet. You still have to eat. You can't have had any decent meals since you left New York. The roadhouse food at the train stops is bad, at best. Besides, I don't want you to fall into the clutches of

Mr. Butler. He does not appear to be one that is easily deterred."

"Well, I…."

"Good, it's settled." He linked her arm through his.

"Forgive the buckboard. I was expecting there to be more baggage."

"Nothing to forgive," said Maggie. "Had things worked out correctly there would have been a trunk."

Caleb simply nodded.

She looked up at the man whose arm she held. Caleb. When did she start thinking of him as Caleb? During one of the dozen times she read every letter he sent? Or when she reread all of them during the long trip here?

"Where are you taking me, Mr. Black?"

"To the Hotel Melvin and the best food in town. I have two rooms there. I had one for Miss Talbot but you can use it now."

"That's very kind of you, considering all that's happened."

"It's the least I can do for the woman I'm going to marry."

"I wish you'd stop saying that. You know it's impossible." Regardless of how charming and handsome he was, she was not going to fall for pretty words again.

"I know no such thing. I intend to convince you of the validity of my suit."

She shook her head. "Mr. Black—"

"Caleb."

"I'm sorry. What?"

"My name is Caleb."

"Caleb," she said liking, the sound of it. It was a strong, steady name. "You know this can't happen."

"Look, you need a room where you can refresh yourself after your long trip. Order a bath if you like. And you need to eat. You might as well come with me."

"I don't know," she said but she kept walking, the mention of a bath won her over.

He smiled.

They reached the end of the platform and his buckboard wagon. He set her bags in the back, held her hand, helped her to climb up onto the bench, steadied her with his other hand at her waist. Then he went around the back to the other side of the wagon and climbed up next to her. Picking up the reins he slapped them down on the horse's behinds. "Giddy up."

Maggie turned and quietly observed him. Dark brown hair curled slightly over the top of his collar. His Stetson rode low on his head leaving his eyes, those beautiful chocolate eyes, in shadow. He wore a dark chambray shirt that appeared to be new and brown wool trousers with well worn boots. The sleeves on the shirt were rolled up in homage to the heat and leather work gloves covered his large, and she remembered, warm hands. Hands that, though rough, were gentle when he touched her.

She rather liked him, despite his high handed ways, having gotten to know him through his letters. She knew he was a widower and had a seven-year-old daughter named Rachel. His wife,

Ruth, had died giving birth and he'd raised Rachel on his own.

"Do you like what you see?" he asked her, having caught her staring at him.

Maggie clasped her skirt a little tighter and ignored his question. "So, Caleb, where is Rachel? She didn't come with you."

He laughed. "I tried to get her to come, but she said she had chores she'd rather do. Most days I can barely get her to do her chores but today she suddenly wants to. She's been getting ready. Decorating for her new mother."

"She's excited? I actually expected the opposite, that she would be anxious about meeting your new wife. Perhaps even resentful."

He nodded. "She's excited and anxious. But she's looking forward to 'having another woman in the house.' Her words, not mine. Anyway, you wouldn't want her to go through all that anxiety for nothing now, would you?"

"I'm not marrying you. As much as I may like you—"

"Ah ha! See, you do like me. I knew it."

She shook her head back and forth. "I didn't
...."

"Yes, you did." He laughed again. She liked the sound of it. It was rich, deep and made her want to smile with him. "You can't take it back now."

She smiled. "You're incorrigible."

"And proud of it, if it gets me what I want and I want you, Maggie."

"Margaret," she said automatically.

"Nah. That's much to staid a name for a fiery redhead like you. Maggie fits much better."

"My family always called me Maggie," she admitted.

"Then how in the world did you start going by Margaret?" It sounded like the name left a bad taste in his mouth.

"My husband insisted. He said Maggie was too common."

"Sounds like a self-righteous bastard to me."

"He was. Edgar always did put on airs."

"Why'd you marry him?" His voice soft, he

asked. "Were you in love?"

She shook her head. "Good Lord, no. I don't think I ever loved him or he me. When he died I wasn't hurt. I was angry…and relieved."

"Angry for him dying?"

"No. That I did everything in my power to make the marriage work and that he was a liar, a cheat and a…" she couldn't say it, couldn't admit what Edgar had really put her through. "You see, he died in his mistress's bed. He embarrassed me and left me in debt." Her hands formed fists of their own accord. Even after five years, anger still radiated through her. Good thing the bastard was dead or they might have arrested her for murder. "By the time I got the creditors paid, all I had left was the one building that I live and work in. I had to sell all of our other assets. I was angry that he left me so few choices. I could sell the building that was left and go back to the farm, to my parents, or try and start my business. I refused to live under my father's thumb again, I chose my business. And, until this," she pointed back and forth between her and Caleb. "fiasco, I've done well at it."

Caleb seemed to ignore most everything she said and honed in on one small fact. "You're a country girl then? How'd you meet your husband?"

He was easy to talk to and he kept her talking. She found herself telling him things she hadn't told anyone before.

"He was passing through on his way to Albany and stopped to ask for directions. He told my father that very day he'd like permission to court me. And he did, for two years, until I turned eighteen. Then he asked my father if he could marry me. Father wanted the match and agreed. Edgar took me to live in New York City and I haven't see my parents or siblings since. He sent them money every month so I guess I was a *bought* woman."

"How did he court you if you lived in the country and he was in the city?"

"With letters mostly. The most beautiful letters and poetry. He was very good with words. And he came by the farm a couple of times a year."

"We've already corresponded for months now.

You know all about me," said Caleb.

He slapped the reins again and the horses, a pair of dappled grays, moved a little faster. They'd been traveling about fifteen minutes and the traffic was so heavy they'd gone only a couple of blocks, if they were lucky.

"I won't be fooled again by beautiful letters. Edgar wrote wonderful letters, none of which hinted at the monster...," she stopped, shook her head and took a deep breath. "I've worked too hard to build my business and I'm not willing to give it up," said Maggie.

He looked at her, the furrow between his brows hinted at the questions she knew he wanted to ask, but he said, "I'm not asking you to give it up. You can move it to Golden."

"Why would I do that? What in the world can you give me I don't have?"

"A home."

"I have a home."

"A family. You need to have a family, Maggie. I can see you have a lot of love in you. It's not good for a woman like you to be alone."

"What makes you think I don't have someone waiting for me back in New York?"

"You wouldn't be considering my offer if you did."

"I'm not considering your offer. It's ridiculous," she insisted.

"Sure you are, or you wouldn't be coming to supper with me."

She didn't know what to say. She was considering it. Tired of living alone, she was lonely. Even when Edgar had been alive she'd often been lonely. It was different now that he was dead. There were no social occasions, no parties or dinner with friends. They'd all disappeared after his death. They were his friends, not hers. All she had now was her business, dinners alone and a cold, lonely bed. But, she also didn't have the beatings every month when she didn't get pregnant or when he came home drunk or just when he felt like it. She could put up with the loneliness.

"I'm not going to marry you. As you said, I

have to eat. That's why I'm going to supper with you. That's all. You are my client and we're going to talk business."

He smiled, a brilliant smile revealing straight, white teeth and an adorable dimple in his right cheek. "If you won't marry me, then I'll have to ask for a refund. Now. I need a wife, Maggie."

"I don't have that much money with me."

"Then I must insist you marry me."

The small smirk on his face told her he thought he'd won. She ignored him. "I won't marry you but I do feel responsible and I have a compromise. I'll acquire an office in Golden and continue to work to get you a suitable wife. In the mean time, I will come and do all the things, within reason, that you need a wife to do. I will do your cleaning and help with your daughter, but I don't cook."

"You work out of the house except for interviews, then we go together to Golden. I don't want you meeting these men alone. I intend to marry you Maggie."

"That's crazy. I won't marry you or anyone

ever again."

"We already know each other, Maggie," he said as he pulled to a stop behind the hotel along with the other wagons and carriages parked there. He jumped off and came around to help her down. Once she was steady, he grabbed her valises with one hand, placed his other hand at her waist and guided her into the hotel to the registration desk where she signed in and received her key.

"Your room is next to mine. I reserved the rooms for two nights, in anticipation of getting to know Miss Talbot a bit before we married."

"How very considerate of you."

He shrugged his shoulders. "I wanted to make sure we suited and were looking for the same things before we married. I have a seven-year-old to consider."

"Of course," she nodded. "What about Rachel? What will she think when you come home with me instead of the *young* woman she's expecting?"

"She's not expecting any particular woman. I haven't told her much. I didn't want to get her hopes up in case it didn't work out with Miss Talbot."

Maggie was suddenly shy about this and about herself. "How can you be sure this is what you want?"

They were walking in the hall of the second floor when he stopped in front of her room. He set her bags on the floor. "Maggie, look at me." She lifted her gaze and clashed with his coffee colored eyes. "I've wanted you since our third letter. I could sense your fire, your vibrant lust for life in every word you wrote. Why do you think I bothered to write after establishing correspondence with my intended? I wrote to *you,* Maggie. You."

She lowered her lashes and looked at his hands clasped with hers. "I always wrote to you, too. I've never shared so much of myself with anyone else," she whispered. "But that doesn't matter. I won't marry again."

"Why? What are we waiting for, Maggie?"

"I'm going to find you a wife. Someone other than me."

"We'll see.."

He hadn't mentioned love. Just as well, she wouldn't have believed him anyway. Though she could easily fall for him. Maybe already had. Was that the real reason she came on the trip? She could have telegraphed him that she needed to find another person to accompany Jenny, but she hadn't. She'd packed her bags and was actually thrilled at the prospect of meeting him.

She made a spur of the moment decision. One she hoped she wouldn't regret. "Very well, Caleb. I'll come to your ranch. I'll live there and work until I find you a bride. But…"

"There's always a but," he grumbled.

"You have to be open to a match."

"I'm open to the right match." He took both her hands in his. "Let's go in your room."

Looking around, she only then realized they were standing in the hallway. "Yes, of course."

She held the door as they entered the room. He set her bags down just inside the door and then took her into his arms. She stiffened. He brought her flush against his body. His aroused body.

"I'm going to kiss you, Maggie."

She looked up at him. "Don't warn me, just do it."

And he did. He kissed her long and slow. His lips teased and then devoured her. His tongue played at the seam of her lips and she opened for him and gave as much as she got. It had been so long since anyone had kissed her. Edgar never kissed her like this. With his whole body. His whole being. And Caleb would allow nothing less than the same back from her. Everything. Everything was in the kiss.

She finally pulled back and sucked air into her oxygen starved lungs.

He seemed no better off, taking deep breaths to replace the air lost during their explosive kiss.

He rested his chin on the top of her head, his fingers still tangled in her hair. "You could be the death of me, Maggie."

"Or you me." She pulled away, went to the bed and sat down, her right hand to her throat. Her heart beat like a drum against her palm.

Caleb sat on the bed next to her and took her left hand in his. He turned it over and kissed the inside of her wrist, then flicked his tongue out and tasted her.

Suddenly she forgot that she was out of breath. All she felt was the pull on her womb from the little touches he gave her.

"My God, Caleb." Her head fell back and she allowed herself to feel all the sensations his touch wrought from her. It had been so long. She needed this, wanted this. But like all things she wanted, the price was too high. She couldn't allow anyone to have that kind of power over her again. She couldn't take the chance. Slowly, she raised her head and looked into his beautiful eyes.

"Maggie." His voice sounded strained.

She shook her head. "No. Caleb. Please. Let me freshen up and then let's just go have dinner. I'll have my bath after dinner. I'm too hot, dirty and tired to think about this now."

"You're right." He backed away, turned and

opened the door. "I'll be back in a few minutes to pick you up."

"Thank you."

Dinner was actually very nice. Caleb ordered for both of them. They each got a hefty portion of pot roast with carrots, turnips, onions and potatoes. It was served with rolls and butter. Simple but wonderful, the beef so tender it melted in her mouth. She hadn't realized just how hungry she was until she put that first bite into her mouth. Then it was hard for her to stop and talk. She just wanted to eat.

This seemed to amuse Caleb. "I haven't met a woman with a good appetite until now."

"It's not that my appetite is so big as much as it is that I haven't had a decent meal in more than a week. And this is wonderful. You said that the food here was good. You weren't kidding."

They talked about everything except the real reason that Maggie was there. Finally, she broached the subject. "I'm sorry that I didn't have Jenny with me. If there was anything I could have done, I would have. But she seemed very much in love and very determined to marry him."

"I understand. I was young once myself."

"Yes, well, I think before we get too involved in this conversation, I must put it off and get my bath. I'm really rather exhausted and need to get some rest."

"That you do. You looked like you've been rode hard and put away wet."

"What?" she stared at him. "I what?"

"Sorry." The pink flush spread up his neck. "It's an expression we use. It just means you look wrung out."

She sighed, put her napkin on the table and rose. "Well, that's as good an expression as any then, isn't it? I am wrung out and a bath and a good night's sleep will do wonders to revive me."

Caleb stood, too, and they left the dining room. He walked her to her room and didn't ask to come in.

"I'll leave you to your bath and see you in the morning."

"Thank you. Good night, Caleb."

"Good night. Sleep well." He turned on his heel and went to the room next door.

Maggie entered her room, locked the door and headed to the bathroom. It had a large claw foot tub, wash stand and privy. She turned on the water and let it run into the tub filling it with water as hot as she could stand. Then she lowered herself into it. She let out a loud sigh as she leaned back and rested, only her neck and head remained out of the steaming liquid.

Half an hour later, she rose out of the now cool bath and dried off with the large bath towel and put on her nightgown and robe. She felt renewed. Ready to take on the world. And she would have to when she saw Caleb in the morning. As much as he amused her, as much as he set her heart a-flutter, it just was not possible. Maggie might enjoy Caleb Black, appreciate many qualities of the man but...but. It was just couldn't work. No. She could not be his bride, bear his name...have his children. Tempting. Oh heavens. Caleb might have well been dangling a carrot. A husband, a friend, a daughter. A home. Someplace safe. But no. Maggie had learned there was no safe haven in marriage. Even in death, the bastard exerted his terror with her thinking. Five years. She was free. or rather, she should be. Instead, his horrible abuse and manipulation made her want to run far and fast from the fine Mr. Caleb Black.

Frustrated, she rubbed her stiff neck. Not just Mr. Black. This was going to be a problem in any companionship she may seek. That fear. That niggling doubt leading to careful words and careful steps. No. Nuptials to anyone was out of the question. Maggie had built a well respected, profitable business that was hers and hers alone.

The building, its units. That was hers. Won with each vicious blow to her stomach. No man would take away what she had earned. No man would again take away or limit her choices. No man would force his will on her or strike her in anger. Not that all would, but that damned marriage license made some men crazy. Another excuse to treat a woman like chattel. Property. That means he can pretty much do anything.

Slow tears ran down Maggie's cheeks. She didn't bother knocking them away. She learned firsthand how true, how literal, how devastating being sold into a marriage, trapped by a binding contract of law could be.

No. No matter who it was, there were to be no weddings in Maggie's future.

She couldn't. Ever. Regardless of anything she may have felt toward Caleb, her fear of marriage was greater.

CHAPTER 2

Maggie had second and third thoughts by morning. She'd tossed and turned all night, going over the pros and cons of her decision. She knew Caleb, probably better than she'd ever known Edgar in their twelve years of marriage. A marriage that didn't include children. Edgar always blamed her and beat her for it. An involuntary shudder wracked her body as she remembered the beatings.

She entered the dining room for breakfast. Caleb was already there, a cup of coffee on the table in front of him. For some reason, the room looked bigger in the light of day. The floor to ceiling flowered wallpaper seemed less yellow and more cream colored in the bright morning light. Brilliant white tablecloths covered the round tables and a small vase of wild flowers sat in the middle of each. Most of the tables seated four people, some more and some, like the one where Caleb sat, seated only two.

He smiled when he saw her, stood to pull out her chair. It had been so long since anyone had treated her like a lady and Caleb seemed to do it automatically, as though it was something she deserved. She liked it. Enjoyed being treated like she was special. She started walking toward him. but faltered when she noticed another occupant of the room. Martin Butler. He raised his coffee cup to her in salute.

"What's he doing here?" she whispered when she got to Caleb.

He turned and saw Martin. "I don't know. Just ignore him."

"That's kind of hard to do when he keeps showing up, but I'll try. I've been doing some thinking." She sat down. As soon as she did, the waitress was there.

"What can I get you, Ma'am?"

Maggie looked up into the eager face of a young woman with cornflower blue eyes. She couldn't have been more than sixteen but she wore a thin gold band on her finger and appeared about seven months pregnant.

"Why don't you bring her a cup of coffee, Bertie. By the time you get back she'll have had a chance to look at the menu."

"Sure thing, Caleb." She looked over at Maggie. "Be right back, Ma'am."

"Now you were saying you've been thinking and I'm not sure I like the sound of that," he replied.

"What if I took a place in town? I could still find you a new wife…,"

"That's not the deal. You're going to be my wife, for lack of a better term, until one is found for me. You agreed and I'm holding you to your word. You wouldn't want me to keep you to any lower standards than I would a man, now would you?"

"No. I wouldn't," she admitted.

"Can I ask you a question?" After she nodded he said, "Why didn't you have children?"

She took a deep breath, the memories still fresh even after five years. "Not that it matters but Edgar assured me it was my fault, I'm not so sure. None of his mistresses had children either, and he had more than one. Mistress that is. He wasn't shy about telling me that he had women who wanted him. Now I'm too old. That's another reason I'm *not* the perfect wife for you."

Caleb reached over and put his hand on top of hers. "I'd never cheat on you, Maggie. When I marry, it's for life. I take my vows seriously."

She looked at the man seated across from her. He was everything she'd always wanted in a man. Tall, handsome. If it was possible for her to have children, he could give them to her. If not, well, he already had a daughter and Maggie could help raise her. She had to admit having a family was very appealing.

"Come on. Let's get married. Now. Today.

Let's not wait. You know you want to. Come with me, Maggie. We can start our new life together."

Maggie gazed into those brown eyes and was almost lost. Almost. She had to remain firm. "We are not marrying. Tell me something. What would you have done with Jenny Talbot?"

"Sent her back home." He released her hand and picked up his spoon, becoming intent on stirring his coffee. "My only thought was to get you here. I know that wasn't well done of me, but I was at my wit's end. I could think only of you and you weren't being very helpful. I finally decided on having you accompany Jenny. I'd have found her a husband if she didn't want to go back to New York. There's plenty of men that she might have found more suitable and more her age than me."

"That wasn't very good of you, but at least you're honest and I have to admit, it's fairly flattering to me. But wrong nonetheless," she added. "Why couldn't you have just asked me in your letters?"

"What would you have said?"

Now it was her turn to look down. She felt her color rise. "No."

"Exactly. I couldn't risk it."

Bertie came back with Maggie's coffee. "Now, what can I get for you?"

Her head popped back up as she glimpsed Martin Butler and lost her appetite. "Just some toast with jam, please."

"You need to eat more than that," said Caleb. "That won't keep a bird alive."

"I'm really not hungry." Her eyes drifted back to Martin.

Caleb followed the direction of her gaze. "You can't let him bother you."

"I can't help it. I feel so bad for Beatrice. She never wrote and told me. I don't even know what happened to her."

"I'm sure she's fine. We'll stop and ask Sheriff Wayburn to look into it. Okay?

"Yes, thank you." She took a sip of the coffee the waitress had brought her. "Let's get down to business, shall we? You need a wife and I need to find you one. First, I'll need to establish an office here and travel into town at least once per week. Second, I'll take care of your home but I won't cook."

"Cookie, one of my trail hands, does the cooking now. It's not good but it's edible. And I have a woman who comes in once a week to do laundry. Rachel and I look after ourselves pretty much the rest of the time. We're not the best housekeepers, but we do alright."

"I don't intend to judge you by your housekeeping skills. I'm just trying to figure out what I'm facing. It also gives me a better idea of what you need in a wife. I'm going to make this right, Caleb. I'm going to find you the perfect wife. Now, if you'll meet me in my room in about thirty minutes, I have some arrangements to make."

She rose from the table and walked toward the kitchen. Marching in like she belonged there, she found the cook. A beautiful woman with black hair pulled up into a bun atop her head and one of the more curvaceous figures Maggie'd seen in sometime. She was dressed simply in a black skirt, white blouse and full apron.

"Excuse me? Are you the chef here?"

"I'm not a chef. Only a part-time cook. I do the morning meals. Chef Roberts does the afternoon and evening meals. What can I do for you?" said the woman in lightly accented English. Maggie guessed her to be Italian or French.

"My name is Maggie Selby and I'd like to hire you," she said, coming right to the point.

The woman started laughing. "You. Hire me. Why?"

"Because I can't cook and the position I've found myself in requires a cook. Are you interested or not? It pays twenty dollars a month and room and board. What's your name?"

Maggie watched the woman's eyes light up at the mention of the pay. She realized she might be overpaying but she needed someone now.

"My name is Francesca Lamrona." She cocked her head to one side and narrowed her eyes. "I care for my mother. Would you provide for her as well?"

Maggie wasn't fazed in the least. "You can bring her to live with you and her room and board will be provided, too, but there is no additional salary for her and she will be expected to help you in the kitchen."

Francesca nodded. "You have a deal. When do you want me to start?"

"Tomorrow. I'll send someone here to pick you up. Is that acceptable?"

She nodded again. "Yes. I will see you tomorrow."

They shook on it and Maggie took her leave. This woman could make a good wife for Caleb. He just didn't know it yet. Why did that thought not make her happier?

*****

Caleb's house was a sprawling one story white clapboard. He pulled up to the side and they entered from a porch just off the kitchen. On the porch next to the door, there was a long, skinny table on which sat three basins with pitchers, soap and towels beside them. With so many basins she assumed this must be where his employees washed before coming in for meals. They'd had a similar set up on the farm where she was raised. They didn't have people working for them but Mother wouldn't let anyone in the house before washing after they'd spent a day in the fields. It was so familiar, almost like being back home.

When they opened the door to the kitchen they were greeted by rolling billows of smoke. "Maggie, stay here." Caleb ran inside.

She coughed and went out and off the porch to wait in the yard. And waited and waited for what seemed like forever and Caleb didn't come out. Finally, concern overtook her and she went into the smoking building to find him. He was at the sink, a lid covering a smoking, sizzling skillet. She propped open the door. He'd already opened the window above the sink.

"What happened?"

"Rachel was trying to surprise us by cooking dinner. Unfortunately, she burned the bacon and nearly set the stove on fire with the grease."

It was then Maggie noticed the little girl. She had dark brown hair in two neat braids and brown eyes, with black lashes, full of tears. She blinked and the tears streamed down her cheeks. Maggie felt sorry for her, she looked so forlorn.

"I'm sure it'll be fine. I'm Maggie," she said, holding out her hand to her.

Rachel looked at her hand and then up into her face and started crying harder.

"Oh, honey," said Maggie, taking the girl into her arms. "It's all right. Caleb tell her it's all right."

Rachel had buried her face in Maggie's chest and shook with sobs.

"Ah, Pumpkin it's okay. No lasting harm was done. Look. The fire's out and the only thing burned is the bacon," said Caleb. He opened his arms to his daughter and she ran from Maggie to him. He gathered her close and held her while she cried. Maggie almost started crying herself at the tender scene.

Now that the kitchen was not filled with smoke and she could see it, Maggie had never seen a bigger kitchen in a private home. The one at the hotel was only slightly larger than this one. A large, six-burner stove with a warming shelf along the back, sat along the wall opposite the door where she stood. If she'd been a cook she'd have been in heaven to have such a stove. As it was, Francesca was going to love it.

There were two doors on that same wall. One on either side of the stove. The one between the stove and the icebox, she was sure, led to the pantry and she assumed the second one led to a bedroom for the cook, who would be arriving tomorrow. That was going to be a surprise for Caleb. The woman was beautiful and could cook. Maggie smiled. Caleb didn't stand a chance.

Along the wall to her left was the sink with hand pump below a small window with pretty flowered curtains. There were counters with cupboards above and below on either side of the sink. A large icebox stood at the end of those counters.

The wall to her right had a doorway opening to the rest of the house and a long table was also against that wall. The table had armchairs at both ends and a long bench on either side. It would easily seat sixteen to twenty people.

On the wall, next to the door where they stood, was a long board nailed about six feet from the floor with pegs all along it for coats and hats. It would more than likely be full at each meal summer and winter with hats, if nothing else.

"We generally eat with the men, otherwise, it gets lonely for just me and Rachel in the dining room. We can change that if you prefer."

"No. That's fine. I like the idea of having lots of people around the table after eating alone for so many years. The conversation must be lively," said Maggie.

From behind them came a short, slim woman with beautiful silver hair wrapped into a tight knot at the back of her head. Maggie hadn't heard any one ride up so she must have already been there.

"Clara," he called to the woman. "I've got someone I want you to meet."

Maggie turned and gazed into a pair of the prettiest blue eyes she'd ever seen. They looked like a deep lake she'd been to once on a trip with Edgar. The water around the edges was clear, but the closer to the center it got the darker and bluer it became until the middle where it was so deep it looked black.

"Ah, Miss Talbot?" asked Clara.

"No," said Caleb. He put his arm around Maggie's waist and brought her close. "This is Maggie."

She pushed away from him and glared. "Stop that." Having him hold her only brought about feelings, wants, she could never have.

He just grinned at her.

"Maggie. Well, I'll be! Did you marry the girl or just bring her home for a visit."

"We most certainly did *not* get married," said Maggie.

"Caleb?" Clara narrowed her eyes at him.

"What have you done?"

"Nothing, except make sure I get my money's worth. The woman I was supposed to marry, Miss Talbot, didn't make the whole trip. Maggie here doesn't have the money to refund me, so she's going to work it off."

"Well I was. He conveniently forgot to mention you."

"Not surprising. I try to do a little cooking and cleaning while I'm here but I'm only supposed to do the laundry and now you're here I won't have to do that. I don't mind telling you I only do it to help Caleb until he finds himself a wife. I've got plenty to do on my own place."

Caleb shrugged his shoulders. "I told you I had a woman who does the laundry."

Clara went to Maggie, grabbed her hand and shook it vigorously. "Good to have you here. Caleb has been talking about you."

He cleared his throat and Maggie cocked her eyebrow in question.

"It's nothing," he said. "We'll talk about it

later."

"Papa?" said the little girl. "Is this my new mother?"

Maggie saw that Rachel had coffee colored eyes that matched her fathers. "Um, no, sweetheart. I'm not. I'm Maggie, but I'm here to find a mother for you." Her heart went out to the little girl. She wanted a mother so much.

"Rachel, honey, Maggie is going to be with us for a while and I want you to make her feel at home. She'll be staying in the large guest room next to mine. Maybe you'd like to show her the way and I'll follow with her bags."

Rachel grabbed Maggie's hand, the tears gone replaced by a bright smile Maggie couldn't help returning. Smoke and fire long forgotten. "Come on, I'll show you the way."

Maggie looked over at Caleb, saw the smile on his face and knew she'd been had. She turned to Rachel. "Thank you. I appreciate your help until I can find my way around."

"After that we can go to the barn and see the

new kittens. We almost always have new kittens of one size or another. These are a couple of weeks old and I like them best this size 'cause they like to play." Rachel chattered on about kittens and puppies and all sorts of other baby animals that they had on the ranch. She pulled Maggie along to the bedroom and flung open the door.

"This is our spare room. Papa calls it the guest room but I sometimes play in here. My room's too small for some of the games I like to play. Do you like to play games, Maggie?"

"Uh, I suppose. I haven't played any games in a long time. What kind do you like to play?" Rachel's little hand in hers reminded Maggie what it was like to be small and only worried about who would play with you.

"Well, mostly I just play with my dolls, after I've done my chores, a course. Papa says I got to be 'sponsible and that means" she stopped and concentrated before speaking again. *"Doin' my fair share"* She grinned, obviously happy she'd remembered what her father said.

"Well, he's right. I always had to help around the house when I was growing up, too."

"Do you like to play checkers? Papa plays checkers with me sometimes."

Maggie listened to the child with half an ear while she looked around the room that she would call home for the next few weeks. It would take her that long to get even one bride candidate out here from New York. First, she had to write to Sally, her tenant and sometime assistant. She'd have to oversee the office while Maggie was gone. Luckily, Sally had helped Maggie out before and knew the workings of the business.

Caleb's file was with Maggie, so she'd have to send Sally the information on Cassie Jones, the woman she wanted to come out here. She was taking a big chance that he'd accept another candidate but at least he hadn't already rejected her. She'd have to put an advertisement in the paper for a new set of brides. Sally could help her sift through them and perhaps find one he'd like. Sally had good instincts and Maggie trusted her implicitly.

Rachel tugged on Maggie's hand. "Maggie, do you want to go see the kittens now or not?"

"Why don't you let her get unpacked first, Pumpkin," said Caleb from the doorway. He had Maggie's bags with him.

"Yes, that would be wonderful," said Maggie. "Maybe you can show me around a little later."

The little girl pouted for about a second, then got a bright smile on her face and said, "Okay." She skipped out of the room and down the hall.

"She's got a lot of energy."

"That she does. Where do you want these?"

"On the bed, please."

"There's other things I'd rather do on the bed." He waggled his eyebrows at her.

"Stop that. You're hopeless."

"No," he said soberly. "I'm hopeful. For the first time in a long time. I'm hopeful and I warn you now, I don't intend to give up on you. I'll see the women you present and I'll try to keep an open mind, but I've already seen the one I want and that's you. Your choice for my bride has a lot to live up to."

"Caleb, I...,"

"Shh," he placed two fingers against her lips. "It'll all work out however it's supposed to." He bent down, replaced his fingers with his lips. "You'll see."

She wanted to pull away, stop the kiss, she really did, but her mind and her body warred and her body won. The kiss was soft and gentle. Unlike the first kiss he gave her. There was nothing carnal about this one and yet she felt it more perhaps because it was so chaste.

He pulled back, touched her cheek with his fingertips, then turned and walked out of the room. She sat on the bed, her legs unable to support her and put her fingers on her lips. The heat from his lips lingered. How in the world was she supposed to remain unaffected by him, when every fiber of her being screamed for fulfillment?

Putting aside her feelings, Maggie unpacked her bags, placed them under the bed and went in search of Caleb. They needed to talk. This couldn't continue. He had to stop touching her. It was inappropriate and distracting and she knew if he continued, she would be tempted beyond what she could resist. It had been so long since anyone had touched her gently. Years. Edgar only had sex with her to get her pregnant and when that didn't work, he quit touching her altogether except to beat her. She hated him and was so grateful he was dead.

But now Caleb made her feel all the things she had never felt before. She yearned to feel the gentleness of his touch. Her body hummed to life whenever he was near, and despite her admonishments and after only three days together, she longed for his kisses. It wasn't good that the man from the letters was all too real. Not good for her at all.

She wanted what he could give. Wanted the caring, the family. Wanted his touch all over her body. She ached for him. But like most things she wanted, she couldn't have it. It would be too easy to give in and say yes, but she couldn't. Her conscious wouldn't let her. This was her business. Her reputation was built on her ability to find matches for the men she took on as clients. Those matches did not include her.

Caleb was not to be hers, but another woman's husband. He only thought he wanted her but what he really wanted was the idea of her. The idea of a wife and mother for Rachel and Maggie was just handy, that was all. She had to remember that. One woman was as good as another when they were at hand. She just needed to get another woman at hand. And she had the perfect one in mind. Miss Cassandra Jones. She and Francesca were the last candidates that Maggie was going to present before finally giving up on finding someone for Caleb. Cassandra was a redhead like Maggie, but much younger and slimmer. Cassandra or Francesca, one of them would be perfect. Right, perfect. So why wasn't she happier about her decision?

*****

Maggie found Caleb in the barn with Rachel. They were by one of the stalls. Rachel stood on the middle rail of the gate with Caleb next to her, both looking over the top rail of the gate into the stall.

"What's going on?" asked Maggie as she approached the pair.

Rachel's head popped up and she jumped down and then ran to Maggie. "Come look, come look." She grabbed Maggie's hand and pulled her along.

"Okay, I'm coming," she laughed at the little girl's enthusiasm.

Rachel let go just as they reached the stall. Caleb turned and smiled. "She's a little excited. It's her first birth."

Maggie stood next to Caleb, so close she could smell his scent, a combination of sandalwood and working man. She looked over the rail at a horse and foal. The foal was still on the ground and its mother nudged it with her nose, encouraging it to stand. The little one tried and fell, tried again and wobbled but stayed on all fours.

Rachel clapped her hands. "He did it." She turned to her papa. "Can I name him?"

"Yes, but we have to determine if it's a boy or

girl."

Caleb went into the stall and petted the mare. "Good girl. You did real good, Starfire. What did you give me, now?" He went to the baby horse and checked it out. "We have a colt. What would you like to call him, Pumpkin?"

"Socks. 'Cause he's got white socks on all his legs."

"Socks it is." Caleb came out of the stall and stood by Maggie. "What do you think?"

"I think it's amazing. Look at the little thing. Standing and it's only minutes old." Maggie shook her head and closed her eyes, picturing the birth in her head. "It's incredible. I know you probably see it all the time and it's old hat to you, but to me and" she nodded in Rachel's direction, "and her it's the most remarkable thing we've ever seen."

"It's never 'old hat'. Every birth is special, whether animal or human." Caleb took Maggie's hand. "Come see our other little ones." They followed Rachel to one of the other stalls, the floor of this one covered in straw. In the corner was a litter of kittens with their mama, four gray striped and one solid black.

"Oh, aren't they adorable. How old are they?"

"About four weeks," said Caleb.

Rachel went in, picked up the black one and brought it back to Maggie. "Here," she said as she shoved the kitten at her.

Taking the kitten from the girl, Maggie automatically cradled it in her hands and brought it up to her face. "Look at you. Such a sweetie," she cooed to the little cat. She turned it on its back in one of her hands and rubbed its belly with the other. The kitten kicked with its feet, battling with Maggie's fingers.

She laughed and put him down. He mewed for his mama and then trotted off in the direction of his littermates.

"Thank you. This was fun. Something I haven't had much of in a long time."

"I'm glad. You should laugh more often. I like to hear you laugh." Caleb reached for her, but Maggie backed away. It was like a bucket of cold water and reminded her why she'd sought him out to begin with. "I came to find out where I can work and to get paper and pen. I have to write Sally, my assistant in New York City."

He took the rejection in stride. "You can work in my office. You'll find stationery in the top right hand drawer and there's a pen and ink on the top of the desk."

"Wonderful." She clasped her hands in front of her. "When can I get to town to mail it?"

"We go to Golden on Saturday's. You can mail it then."

"Saturday! But that's three days away. Can't we go sooner? Like tomorrow?"

"Sorry, darlin'. This is a ranch. We have to keep a schedule and Saturday's are set aside for town."

"I get to go to town on Saturday's, too," said Rachel. "It's fun. You'll like it Maggie. They got lots of candy and new dolls at the general store. I like lookin' at 'em, but Papa says I can't touch." She frowned for just a moment and then turned her attention back to the kittens.

"Very well. I'm sure I'll be busy until then."

"Oh, you will." He turned to his daughter. "Pumpkin, will you go find Cookie for me and have him come to the house, please?"

"Sure. I know right where he is," she replied and ran for the door. "In the bunkhouse, sleeping it off."

She was gone before Maggie could say anything. Instead she looked at Caleb and raised her eyebrows.

"Cookie has a little problem. But he's harmless."

"Harmless? It's not good for a child to witness that kind of behavior."

He advanced on her. "You can tell me lots of things. How to raise my daughter isn't one of them."

He reached for her. She flinched and closed her eyes.

"Maggie?"

She opened her eyes and saw the questioning

look on his face and realized what she'd done. It was still ingrained in her...preparing for the beating that followed when Edgar reached for her. She shook herself.

"It's nothing. You're right, I shouldn't tell you how to raise Rachel. She's a wonderful little girl and a testament to you. She has so much energy. How do you keep up?"

Caleb was still staring at her. He narrowed his eyes but answered the question. "I'm not sure I do. I think I just tag along in her wake and try to keep her from hurting herself with her curiosity."

"Well," said Maggie as she turned toward the door and tried to put some distance between her and Caleb. "Do you want to show me the rest of the house and your office?"

"I'd rather kiss you." He'd come up behind her and put his hands on her upper arms. He brought her back flush to his chest and held her ever so gently.

She stiffened and pulled away. "Caleb. We can't. Please."

He let her go. "I'm not going to pretend with you. I intend to marry you, Maggie Selby. One way or another."

She didn't back down. "My name is Margaret," she said defiantly. "And I told you, I will never marry again."

.

CHAPTER 3

Knock. Knock. Knock.

Maggie's eyes popped open and she sat up. Moonlight from the open window fell on a room that was unfamiliar. She was lying on a brass bed. Next to it was a nightstand with an oil lamp and one of her books on it. She vaguely remembered trying to read it last night.

Across the room stood a wardrobe and a tallboy dresser both in a dark wood, maybe cherry. She swung her legs over the side of the bed. They landed on an oval shaped braided rug on the floor next to the bed. It protected her feet against the morning chill that raised goose bumps on her arms.

The knocking came again. "Maggie. It's me, Caleb. Wake up."

Then it hit her. She'd agreed to fill in for the wife she was supposed to bring him.

"Yes. I'm coming." She lit the lamp so she had more than moonlight to see by. Pulling on her robe, she went to the door. Opening it just a crack, she asked, "What do you want this early?"

Caleb pushed open the door and walked in. "Time for you to earn your keep. I've got ten hungry men that are going to want breakfast in about an hour and a half. You better get cooking." He went to the wardrobe and pulled out a plain black dress. "Don't you wear anything but black and white?"

Maggie grabbed the dress from him. "You can't just barge into my room like that. I insist that you leave. Now." She pointed at the door.

"I knocked first and waited until you answered. Now, I've got a dress. If you want, I'll be your ladies maid." He waggled his eyebrows at her. Then something in the closet caught his eye. He brought out her light blue dress. "Is this the blue dress you told me about in your letters? The one that chafes your neck and leaves it raw for days? Why would you bring that with you? Why would you keep it if it hurts you?"

"That's none of your business." She snatched the dress from him. She shoved at his chest, backing him toward the door. "Go. Get out. I'll go to the kitchen shortly, and you'll get the one and only meal I'm cooking. Scrambled eggs and biscuits."

He laughed and then he took her hand and brought it to his lips. Just as he was about to kiss it he turned it over and kissed the inside of her wrist. All the while he kept his eyes on her. It was the sexiest thing anyone had ever done to her and she felt the rush of heat to her core.

When she regained her wits, she noticed he was looking at her and smiling. With little resistance, he let her push him out. She closed the door and leaned back against it. He remembered what she'd written to him. Something trivial and he'd remembered it. She was genuinely touched.

The man was going to be the death of her. She had to admit, she liked his playful nature. Edgar didn't have a playful side even when they were first married. He'd been staid and serious from day one. Maybe it was his age, but she figured he'd always been that way. Stodgy. Dry. Old.

Caleb was young. There was nothing stodgy about him. He was only forty and virile, vibrant. He loved life. She could tell by the way he treated Rachel, the way he treated Maggie. She shook herself. The man was like candy, hard to resist. This was business, just business, and she had to remember that.

She put the blue dress back in the closet, knowing she wouldn't have brought it if she'd had anything else. She wasn't one to spend a lot of money on clothes. She had three serviceable dresses. The black one, a brown one and the light blue one. It was the prettiest of the dresses and she'd brought it for Sunday services.

She donned the black dress he'd pulled out of

the closet. It was her most serviceable for the work she was about to do. It had been a long time since she'd cooked for a crowd, but she was up to the task. On the farm, as a child, it wasn't unusual to cook for thirty people during harvest season. This should be a piece of cake.

Caleb was already in the kitchen. He turned and smiled at her when she entered. "Ready to work, I see. Clara's got aprons hanging on the inside of the pantry door." He went on about making coffee. There was already one pot brewing on the huge six burner stove. The stove was coal fired and he had most of the burners going.

"I've lit the stove. I wanted it hot for you and wasn't sure you knew how to light one. I'll go gather the eggs and milk the cows for you. That's something you'll want to add to your list of chores."

"Hmpft," she said as she tied the apron around her. "I saw the makings for biscuits in the pantry. Tell me again how many people we need to feed?"

"Including you, me and Rachel, there are usually thirteen mouths to feed. There's only twelve today. My foreman is up at the summer pasture and won't be back until later. Oh, and don't be fooled into thinking Rachel won't eat much because she's a child. She has a big appetite. I think she's in a growth spurt. Speaking of which, do you sew?"

"No. Not very well. I can sew on a button, that's about it. Why?"

"Just thought you might be able to alter her clothes as she grows. It doesn't matter. There's a Chinese laundry and tailor in Golden who's been doing it for years now."

Maggie put the flour, baking powder, lard, and buttermilk out on the counter. Then she got out the rashers of bacon and put them in the huge cast iron skillets to cook. She started to mix together the biscuit dough and get it ready to roll out. "I'm not going to be here long enough for her to grow out of any of her clothes."

"We'll see."

She blew a stray hair out of her face. "We won't see. I'm going to have you a wife long before Rachel needs new clothes. I'm very good at what I do."

Caleb plucked the egg basket from the counter. "And I'm very patient when I need to be. I'm prepared to be patient for you." He raised his hand to her face. "You have flour on your nose." He brushed it off and then bent down and kissed her nose.

"Why'd you do that?"

"It was just too adorable to resist. Just like the rest of you. Too adorable to resist. If you'd give me the chance, we'd make a great couple." He closed the distance until their bodies were flush together. "Want to take the chance? Live a little?"

She pushed him away and turned back to the counter. "No. I don't. I can't."

He shook his head and went out the door. Then he turned back. "Don't think I'm giving up."

"And don't think I'm giving in," she called to his back. She rolled her eyes and finished the biscuits. Then she prayed for patience and stamina. She had to remain firm and get Francesca and Miss

Jones here as soon as possible. One of them was the perfect bride for Caleb. She sucked the right side of her lower lip into her mouth. This was the right thing. Finding him a bride was the right thing to do. It was what she did, what she was good at. So, why did this feel so wrong?

Her breakfast that morning was a success. She'd put the bacon, eggs and biscuits on the table along with chokecherry jelly she'd found in the pantry. Everything was eaten quickly and though the men were polite enough not to say anything, they probably could have eaten twice as much if she'd have fixed it. Francesca would be arriving today and she'd be doing all the rest of the cooking. She'd have to mention that the men had *big* appetites.

Caleb had been right about Rachel. She ate nearly as much as some of the men. Maggie didn't know where she put it, the girl was thin as a rail.

After breakfast, Maggie went to Caleb's office to do her correspondence. She wrote to Sally first.

Dear Sally,

In my apartment, in the sugar container is fifty dollars. After contacting Miss Cassandra Jones and getting her signature on the contract, use thirty-five dollars of the money to purchase tickets for Miss Jones to Denver. Then start interviewing new clients. I need you to keep the business going until I return.

I'm thinking to start an office here in Golden. Would you be amenable to becoming a full time employee and handling the office there in New York City? We can discuss the particulars at a later date after you've had a chance to think it over and discuss it with Henry.

Please write me as soon as you get confirmation from Miss Jones that she is willing to come out here. There is no guarantee that she will marry the client here, but if that be the case, then I will find another husband for her and get her lodgings until that time.

Sincerely,

Margaret

Satisfied with the letter, she let it dry then put it in an envelope she'd already addressed. Saturday was a long way off but in the scheme of things she supposed it didn't matter. It would be three weeks before Miss Jones could be here anyway so an extra day or two didn't make a difference.

Maggie sat back and contemplated her next course of action. She had to continue the work on the ranch, but she also needed to start her new business in Golden. There were lots of ranchers and miners who wanted and desperately needed wives and many women desperate to start a new life.

She wouldn't be able to look for space to rent or anything else until Saturday. It would take nearly all of the fifty dollars she had with her to get another place going. Maybe Caleb was right and for now she should work out of the house to save money. She would be there anyway, might as well take advantage of the situation. After his contract was resolved, she'd look for new lodgings for both herself and her business.

First, she needed to write an advertisement. She glanced at the clock on the corner of Caleb's desk. No, first she needed to find out where Francesca was. Maggie had asked one of Caleb's cowboys to fetch her and she should arrive at any time.

She went out to the front porch and looked down the long driveway to the main road. She saw a buckboard traveling slowly up the driveway. Good. Caleb was in for a surprise. Not only would there be good food on the table but the cook was a feast for the eyes. As they pulled up, Maggie noticed a lone horse and rider behind the buckboard. Martin Butler.

She waited until both the buckboard and Martin had drawn to a stop in front of the house.

"What are you doing here, Mr. Butler? How did you find me?" asked Maggie.

"I followed you yesterday until I saw where you were going. Today, I saw that cook woman pack up and get in this here wagon. I 'membered you talkin' to her yesterday and took a chance and follered her. Guess the chance paid off."

"Well, you can just turn around and leave. You're not wanted here. Our contract was fulfilled. You got the bride you contracted for. The fact that she left after seeing you is your fault and your problem, not mine. If you had been honest to begin with, we could have found you a bride that would have been more agreeable."

"If I wanted a floozy for a wife, I could have married one a long time ago."

"You stop disrespecting Mrs. Selby," shouted the gray haired woman seated next to Francesca on the buckboard bench.

"Now, Mama, it is not our place to interfere."

"Tsk. Shame on you. It is always our place to say something to protect our employer."

"You just keep your trap shut, you ole biddy," said Martin to the woman, using his legs and his reins to try to steady his horse who pranced around because of all the shouting.

"You will not speak to me like that, you *vecchia poiana*."

"What'd you call me? That weren't no English."

"That Mr. Smart Joe was Italian. And I call you, how you say, an old buzzard." The little woman smiled from ear to ear.

"Mama, please," pleaded Francesca as her mother climbed down off the wagon and marched over to Martin Butler's side.

The woman poked Martin several times in the thigh with her finger, punctuating each word she said. "You. Will. Apologize."

"I won't. You ole cow," said Martin, eyes only for the small woman poking him. He grabbed her hand and held it.

"Then you will leave. Now." Maria stamped her foot, finally, pulled her hand away and pointed the way he'd come.

"He will leave now, whether he apologizes or not," said Maggie. She didn't miss the interaction between Francesca's mother and Martin. Though they shouted at each other, they never took their eyes off each other, either. There was an attraction there, or Maggie would give up matchmaking.

Caleb came around the corner of the house. "You listen to the ladies, Butler, and get off my property."

Martin finally looked up and directly at Caleb. "I'm leavin' Black, but I'll be back. Margaret Selby is gonna marry me and make things right or give me back my money."

Maggie came down off the porch and stood next to Mrs. Lamrona. "I'll be doing neither. I fulfilled my part of the contract. You lied and voided the agreement."

"Get going, Butler. Now. Before I have my men commence to filling you with lead."

Maggie looked around her. On either side of the house were two men, four all together, each of them armed, guns drawn.

"You're not really going to kill him, are you?" she whispered to Caleb.

"If he doesn't leave in the next thirty seconds, I'll have him shot for trespassing. The sheriff won't have any trouble seeing it my way since he's on my property." Caleb's hand rested on the Colt revolver at his side.

Martin turned his horse. "I'm leaving, but I'll be back. I'll get what's coming to me." He galloped down the driveway and onto the main road. Everyone stayed where they were until he was out of sight. Then it was a free for all, everyone talking at once.

"You must be Francesca's mother. I'm Maggie Selby," she held her hand out.

"Maria Lamrona," said the little woman as she took Maggie's offered hand and pumped it excitedly. "Thank you for giving this job to my Francesca. Getting out of the hotel is wonderful for us and the money, it is very generous. "

"What do we have going on here, Maggie?" Caleb walked up to the three women. Francesca had climbed down and joined her mother and Maggie.

"Caleb, this is Francesca Lamrona and her mother, Maria. Francesca is your new cook." Maggie crossed her arms over her chest and dared him to nay say her.

"Welcome, ladies." He tipped his hat toward Francesca and her mother. "I'm sure Maggie will make you right at home."

Maggie looked at him and her jaw dropped. She'd expected an argument. Not his nonchalant acceptance of her decision.

Caleb reached over and nudged her mouth closed. "You've really got to stop doing that. You're going to start catching flies." He smiled and walked back the way he'd come, whistling while he went.

Maggie showed Francesca and her mother to the bedroom off the kitchen. "Here you go, ladies. I had the single beds moved in from one of the other bedrooms. I thought you'd be more comfortable than together in a double bed."

"That was very thoughtful of you. It's lovely and please, call me Fran. Only my mother uses Francesca."

"There is nothing wrong with your name," said Maria. "It is the name we gave you, your father and

I, God rest his soul." She crossed herself. "It is what I will always call you, not this *Fran*."

"Yes, Mama." Fran rolled her eyes and sighed. "We are in America now. We should do things like Americans."

"Just because we are in America does not mean we should forget who we are," said Maria, her Italian accent seeming particularly heavy with these words.

Maggie didn't want to get into the middle of this. "Well, I'll leave you to unpack. Dinner is in three hours. Help yourself around the kitchen. You know as much about it as I do. I only arrived yesterday myself."

"You are not the missus?" asked Fran.

"No. I'm a matchmaker. I was hired to find Mr. Black a wife and when that didn't work out properly, I was trapped...er...offered to fill in until I find him the proper bride."

Fran's eyes lit up. "Mr. Black is not married and looks for a wife? He is very handsome."

Maggie shrugged. "Yes, I suppose if you like

that rugged type."

*****

Maggie took the buckets of hot water and put one beside each basin on the long table on the porch. Then she stepped over to the huge triangle and ran the metal rod around the inside of it. The din was nearly overwhelming but there was no doubt everyone heard it.

Rachel and her father showed up first followed closely by the rest of the men. They all politely waited until Rachel had gone into the kitchen before they got too boisterous. Then they started laughing, pushing each other, telling jokes and generally acting like men. Maggie had begun to wonder if any of them were rowdy but apparently they were, just not around Rachel. Although she would bet Rachel could cuss with the best of them. No matter how hard they tried, they couldn't hide who they were from her completely. After all, they *were* men. She remembered from her own days growing up on the farm exactly how colorful their language could be.

Francesca's meal was wonderful and Maggie was glad she'd hired her.

"Papa, can I go outside and play?"

"Yes, you may." He smiled at his daughter as she shot out the door, nearly knocking him over in the process. "Whoa, Pumpkin, slow down," he called to her retreating form as she whizzed past.

Maggie couldn't help but laugh. "The girl is a whirlwind."

"That she is," Caleb agreed. "Are you ready to see the rest of the ranch?"

"I am."

Francesca walked over to them. "I did not mean to overhear but I would like to see the ranch as well, if that is alright. I need to know where things are so I can do my chores. Do you mind if I come with you?"

"Not at all," said Caleb. "How can I mind accompanying two beautiful women around my property?"

"Mama, will you start on supper? We'll have a stew with the meat in the icebox."

Her mother nodded and said, "You all go on. I'm fine here."

"Shall we?" Caleb held the door for both women and then when they were outside he put his elbows out for each of them to take an arm.

"You've a lot of buildings here," said Maggie as she put her arm through his.

"No more than most ranches around here. There are eight buildings on the property. The house and barn, which you're already familiar with." He winked at her and she felt the blood rush to her face. "And then there's the bunkhouse where the cowboys live. The chicken coop, ice house, pump house, the coal shed and last, there's the foreman's cabin on the south ranch which you can't see from here."

"Well, if I'm going to start helping you around here, I guess I better find out where things are," said Maggie.

"Me, too," Fran chimed in.

As they crossed the yard, arm in arm, Caleb pointed out the pump house and the ice house.

"The coal shed is around the corner on the back side of the house. You can't miss it."

Fran nodded. "I'm sure I'll find it when I need it."

"Next to the coal shed is the wood pile for the fireplaces. I also keep some wood on the porch off the kitchen and out of the weather."

"I noticed that," said Maggie. "That's a good idea. Do you get a lot of snow here?"

"It snows pretty regular in the winter, but most of the time, it melts in the next few days. Occasionally, we'll have a blizzard that'll last a day or two and then the snow stays on the ground longer. But in general, the weather's good. We get lots of sunshine, usually some every day."

They continued to walk and the chicken coop was the next structure they came to. Caleb led them inside. There were three rows of nests, one above the other, with eight nests per row. There was plenty of room to walk behind the rows.

"Very nicely set up. It'll make gathering the eggs much easier," said Maggie.

"That's the idea. Normally, it's Rachel's job but I've been letting her sleep in. She's been so excited about you...er...my new wife coming, it's been hard for her to get to sleep."

Maggie looked at him and raised her eyebrow. "You told her about me?"

He looked contrite. "Maybe a little."

She took a deep breath and calmed herself. "I'm not going to talk about this right now other than to tell you that you have to make sure that Rachel understands I won't be staying. I don't want her to be hurt." Of all the people who could be hurt, it was Rachel that upset her the most. Maggie knew how much the little girl wanted a new mother and she didn't want Caleb to get her hopes up that it would be Maggie.

"I'll make sure."

Cocking her head, Maggie eyed him.

"Honest," he said, crossing his heart.

"All right. Now I'm sure neither Fran nor I mind gathering the eggs, but if it's Rachel's chore then she should get back to it. I don't want her to get into the habit of thinking we'll be doing her chores for her."

"I know. I'll give them back to her in a few days."

The last building before the barn was the bunkhouse. It was a large rectangular building about thirty feet long and at least half that wide.

"This is the bunkhouse. You're not responsible for the upkeep. The boys take care of their own needs. All you have to do is their laundry. Right now Thursdays, are laundry days. Clara will be back tomorrow to show you what to do and to help this first time."

Just as they came to it the bunkhouse door opened and a tall, handsome man, with sandy blond hair, came out.

"Ah, Tom. I see you're back from the summer pasture. Ladies, this is Tom Weatherford, my foreman. This is Maggie Selby and our new cook, Francesca Lamrona."

"Mrs. Selby," he said taking her hand. "Pleased to finally meet you."

Maggie's gaze shot to Caleb's. "Just how many people did you tell about me?"

"Not many," he said with a smile.

Tom moved in front of Fran and held out his hand. "Mrs. Lamrona."

"Miss and please, call me Fran."

"No. Fran is much too common a name for such a beautiful woman. Francesca is so much better."

Fran blushed prettily.

Maggie watched the exchange between the two. "Well, hell," she said to herself. Fran was clearly smitten with Tom and he with her. She'd seen it happen enough times to know that Fran was definitely out of the running as far as Caleb was concerned. She only had eyes for Tom now.

Caleb watched the exchange between the two of them as well, with a self-satisfied smile on his face. "Tom, why don't you show Fran the barn and corrals? Maybe she'd like to see our latest bunch of horses and the new colt, too."

Tom smiled broadly. "Yes, sir. Be happy to.

Francesca," he held his arm out to her.

Maggie watched them go. "Pretty pleased with yourself, aren't you?" In actuality, she was relieved. She'd imagined Fran and Caleb in bed and it nearly killed her. She was jealous of someone he hadn't even shown any interest in other than to be polite. What was the matter with her? This was her business. Finding brides for men was what she did. This time shouldn't be, couldn't be, any different, but it was. Caleb was different. She knew him. That was her first mistake. Coming out here had been another, but she couldn't change it now. She'd just have to make the best of it.

"As a matter of fact...," he said with a smug smile on his face.

A smile she wanted to wipe off. She swatted his arm. "Show me the rest and don't think you've won. I still have other candidates."

Past the bunkhouse was the barn where she'd seen the kittens and the colt. She hadn't paid much attention to it before, being too intent on finding Caleb. Now she saw that it was a big, red, two-story building with double doors and next to those a regular sized door. Once inside she saw fourteen stalls, seven on either side. At the end of the stalls on one side was a room for tack which he told her included saddles, bridles, extra reins and other items needed by the cowboys to do their jobs. On the other side was a large stall with hay on one side and straw on the other.

"I hope you're not expecting me to clean the stalls, because I won't do it. You can do it or have someone else, or it won't get done."

He laughed. "Feisty this morning aren't we. It's called mucking and no, I don't expect you to muck out the stalls. I do expect you or Fran to milk the cows. We have two. Bessie and Burt."

She burst out laughing. "Bessie and *Burt*?"

He chuckled. "Rachel named them. She was four."

Dabbing at her eyes, tearing from laughter, she said, "I guess it can be forgiven, then."

He moved closer to her, reached out and ran his finger tip along her jaw. "You have a beautiful laugh. I do like it when you laugh." He leaned in to kiss her. "But I like it better when you don't," he said just before his lips claimed hers.

Maggie was lost. Just like every other time he kissed her, she didn't want it to end. Of their own volition, her arms wrapped around his neck and she pulled her body flush with his.

He pulled away, enough to look down at her. "Ah, Maggie, what you do to me. Can you feel it?" He rubbed his erection on her. "All I have to do is look at you, hear your voice, see your smile and I'm ready. Let me love you, Maggie." He started backing toward one of the empty stalls.

Maggie let him lead her, her body aching for what he could give her. But then she stopped, realized what they were about to do, and pulled away.

"No. Caleb, I don't want this. Don't want it this way."

He took a deep breath and dropped her hand. "You're right. I'm sorry. You just do things to me...I haven't felt this way for a long time."

"I know. Me, either. But this isn't the way. For either of us. You'll have a bride here in three weeks time or there about. And once you accept her, I'll be leaving."

"Stay. Live here. Open an office here. There are lots of miners and cowboys that need wives."

She pulled away from him, putting space between their aching bodies. "I'm not marrying anyone ever again. I did that once. Never again."

He could have stopped her but he let her go. "Maggie, I'm not Edgar. Everything I said in my letters was...is...true."

She wrapped her arms around her middle. "You don't understand. I can't...I won't take that chance again." With a sob, she turned and ran from the barn.

*****

Saturday finally came. Maggie had a telegram and her letter ready to send. She hadn't been planning on telegraphing Sally, but the situation with Caleb demanded she get Miss Jones out there as soon as possible. For the sake of her own sanity.

She was much too attracted to him and he wasn't making it easy.

He always found ways to be alone with her. To accidently touch her hand when they reached for the same things at the supper table. Or he'd drop his fork, reach down to pick it up and run his hand up her leg, knowing she couldn't do anything about it. Not that she would have anyway. She liked the feel of his hand on her leg. It made her tingle in places she hadn't ever tingled before. It was disconcerting and…wonderful at the same time.

He'd meet her in the barn at milking time and rub her back while she worked. It felt so good just to have another human being touch her. She found herself milking slower than she would have otherwise just to have it continue.

At night, after dinner, he'd sit with her in his office while she worked on new advertisements or correspondence. She told him things she'd never told anyone else. About her business and why she started it.

"My first tenant in the building I now own was

a young, single woman named Eliza. She was an honest working woman. Doing whatever she could to stay alive. She was a plain girl and had no living family or, as far as I could tell, any friends. She worked as a laundress for fifteen dollars a month and cleaned offices at night for another ten dollars a month. Edgar charged her ten dollars a month for rent on the small, one bedroom apartment on the top floor of the building.

"Eliza wanted to get married in the worst way. She wanted a family and children. She longed for children of her own. Deciding that becoming a mail order bride was the only way for a twenty-five year old woman like herself to find a husband, she answered an advertisement."

"Is that when you decided to become a matchmaker? When Eliza answered the ad?"

"No. Later. Eliza's new bridegroom was a miner in California. She went out on the train and started sending me letters right away. She said her husband was a big, burly man and was generally kind to her but he liked to drink.

"The letters kept getting shorter. She said in one that her husband didn't like her writing to me and then he would get drunk and hit her. He was always apologetic the next day and Eliza accepted his apology."

"That was a mistake. Men like that don't change," said Caleb.

"I know. But in one of the last letters I got, she said her dreams were finally coming true. She was pregnant and expecting in about six months.

"I was afraid for her. Having lived with Edgar for twelve years I knew how the beatings could go and if Edgar had been a real drinker instead of a just a sadist, he could have gotten out of control and killed me easily. I often hoped he would. That he would finally put me out of my misery, but he didn't. He only hurt me enough to keep me to my bed for a few days and he never hit me in the face, only places it wouldn't show."

Caleb came around the desk and knelt in front of her. "Maggie, I'm so sorry."

"There's nothing to be sorry for. You didn't

know me. You couldn't have changed it if you had. He was my husband. He could do to me what he wanted. It was his legal right."

"No wonder you don't want to get married again."

He placed his hand on her knee and she let him keep it there as she continued. It felt safe. "When Eliza's letters suddenly stopped, I feared the worst. After two months and there still had been no letter, I wrote to the local sheriff's office for information. The response was as I feared. Eliza had been killed by her husband in a fit of drunken rage. He was to hang for the crime.

"I decided then and there to do something about it. The mail order bride business didn't appear to be going away any time soon and I thought women shouldn't have to fear for their lives when answering these advertisements. So I started Matchmaker & Co in order to help these girls. By checking out the men, ensuring that they weren't felons, weren't women beaters, I helped the girls and the women to make good matches and to live their lives in safety. I wanted to make sure that what happened to Eliza didn't happen to anyone else."

Caleb rose and pulled a chair up next to her. "I'm impressed by your fortitude and sense of right and wrong. You saw a wrong and worked to change it. Something not a lot of people would even attempt."

Maggie looked down at her hands, now folded in her lap, unused to the praise. "My idea took off. I hired detectives and put advertisements in the local papers in California and the Colorado Territory. Places where there were lots of single men because of the mining operations. Then I placed similar notices in the New York Times, the Herald and the Tribune, advertising for brides. The responses were overwhelming."

"I imagine they were. The ladies would have put great stock in being safe, I would think."

"They appeared to. Once my business practices became known, business tripled and more. I became one of the most successful arrangers of mail order marriages in the Northeast from New York to Boston. Unmarried women flocked to me in the hope of finding a husband and a better life. I helped the men too, by keeping my standards for the women high as well. I didn't accept drug users or prostitutes, though I did try to get those poor souls off the streets."

Caleb listened to her tell the stories of some of the women she helped and the men, too. He knew she'd arranged the marriages, very successful marriages, of his friends John Atwood and Nathan Ravenclaw. Both couples were happy and in love. They'd had new babies in the last year as a result.

He thought he could be happy with Maggie but she knew better. She could never be happy with someone who didn't love her and he'd never once mentioned love.

CHAPTER 4

Miss Cassandra Jones arrived on the 1:15 train from Omaha. He and Maggie were both there to meet her. She could have been Maggie's little sister with the same fiery red hair and a smattering of freckles across her nose. She had clear blue eyes, not Maggie's green ones, but Caleb couldn't help but note she was a lovely girl. That was the problem. She was a girl. Maggie was a woman. Cassandra's slender beauty couldn't compare with Maggie's lush, soft curves. She was a pale imitation without the fire.

"Cassandra," said Maggie, waving to her.

"Maggie," she waved back. "I finally made it.

You wouldn't believe all the things I had to go through. It was awful. I'm never going to make that trip again. I don't care if my husband wants to go to New York or not, I'm not getting on another train again as long as I live." She spoke non-stop and Maggie couldn't get in a word edgewise.

Finally, she said, "Cassandra! Stop. You won't have to go on the train again."

"Well, good. I was worried for a bit."

"I want you to meet Mr. Caleb Black. Caleb, this is Cassandra Jones."

"Mr. Black," said Cassandra, holding her hand out to him.

"Miss Jones, I'm very glad to make your acquaintance," he said, taking her hand. "Maggie has told me a lot about you but I'd rather hear it from you."

"Please call me Cassandra or Cassie. Miss Jones seems too formal considering we may well be marrying each other soon."

"Very well, Cassie. Call me Caleb."

She smiled prettily at him. "Caleb, tell me

about your home."

He perked up at the mention of his ranch. "I own about two thousand acres outside of Golden and run 200 head of cattle. There are ten men working for me and Maggie just hired a cook who came with her mother in tow. I also keep horses, milk cows and chickens. Then, of course, there is my Rachel. She's my pride and joy. I know you'll like her."

"Oh, yes," agreed Maggie, "she's just the sweetest little girl."

"It all sounds quite...large. I'm not used to taking care of so many people," said Cassandra. "Will it take us long to get to your home?"

"Actually, it's going to take several hours. We're way out in the country. We'll be home just an hour or so before supper. But you should have time to freshen up a bit after your trip."

Maggie watched him. His eyes were actually twinkling. He had something up his sleeve, she just didn't know what it was. She was not going to give up nor was she going to put all her hopes on

Cassandra. Now that she saw her again, she didn't know if she'd be a good match for Caleb or not. But she'd decided she was not giving up. She'd start a new search. Sally would have other candidates by now. She'd wire her right away.

"Caleb, I need to send a telegram before we go back home. Sally's going to have to send me some files."

"Home? You said home, Maggie."

"Don't get excited. It's just a figure of speech. I should have said back to your home." She brushed by him in the direction of the buggy. Caleb walked with Cassie and helped her into the back seat along with her bag. Maggie sat next to him in front. She supposed she should have sat with Cassie but she wanted to spend the time with Caleb. Even with Cassie in back, they could still have some private time. Much to her dismay, she was going to miss spending time with him.

Cassie talked continuously. Told them about the trip out from New York and how excited she was when they'd finally announced that Denver was the next stop. She barely stopped for a breath the whole way home. But she didn't seem particularly interested in Caleb, just in being out of New York. Maggie was somewhat relieved by that and that bothered her.

Three weeks had gone by since Tom began to court Fran. Their courtship was progressing nicely and even though it had been such a short time, Maggie was sure Tom was about to propose. She had no doubt that Fran would say yes. At least they wouldn't lose a wonderful cook and foreman. They had already talked about it and Fran would move into his little cabin on the lower ranch. Her mother would stay in the bedroom off the kitchen until an addition to the cabin could be built. Tom had started on it but they wanted to marry before it was finished.

This whole contract with Caleb was a fiasco, but she refused to give up. She'd find him a bride and if it wasn't Cassie, it would be someone else, but it wouldn't be Maggie. She couldn't marry again. As much as she was growing fond of Caleb, she was not the right woman for him. She couldn't be. Could she?

No. Thinking like that could only get her in trouble. He'd never mentioned anything about love. Still, he thought he could convince her to marry him but that was not going to happen. She was never going to let another man have dominion over her. And regardless of how much Caleb respected her, he would be the husband and she would be the chattel. She would have no more rights than his cattle. She couldn't live like that.

"You're awfully quiet," said Caleb. "What's going on in that amazing mind of yours?"

"Nothing. Just thinking about when we get back to the ranch."

He put his hand on her knee and leaned over to whisper in her ear. "You don't have to find another bride. The one I want is right here."

She moved his hand and whispered back. "That's impossible. You know that. I'm not marrying again. I can't."

"Maggie, I'm not Edgar. Surely you realize

that."

"I know. It's not you. I'm sure you would be a kind and gentle husband. If I didn't feel that way, I wouldn't be trying to find you a bride. It's me. I can't give that kind of control over my life to anyone. It takes a leap of faith I'm not willing to make."

She watched sadness replace the sparkle in his eyes. He turned and looked down the road.

"I'm willing to wait Maggie. I don't want another bride. You can bring girls out here until the sun don't shine and I'll still only want you."

She didn't say anything. There was nothing more for her to say.

*****

Caleb had promised to keep an open mind, so maybe when he got to know Cassie, he'd change his mind.

"So Cassie, tell Caleb a little about yourself."

"Certainly. Well, I was the oldest of three children, but my parents and siblings died of influenza, so I'm by myself now. I was raised on a farm and am used to hard work. I was working as a seamstress in New York City and can sew very well." As if realizing why she'd come out on this trip she added, "And what about you, Mr. Black? I know you're a rancher and have a daughter but that's about all."

When Caleb didn't answer fast enough, Maggie poked him in the ribs. "My daughter is everything to me. My wife, Ruth, died when Rachel was born and I've raised her by myself."

"I understand. That is a terrible thing to have to go through, losing someone we love. Losing my family was just as hard, but we both made it, Mr. Black. We cannot live in the past."

"Quite right, Cassie. Quite right. So what else do you like to do?"

Maggie shook her head and rolled her eyes in frustration as Caleb deftly turned the conversation from himself. He wasn't going to make this easy. But then he hadn't said he would, only that he would keep an open mind. How did you tell if someone had an open mind about something?

He was right about one thing; they arrived at the ranch just an hour before supper. She showed Cassie to the small bedroom next to Rachel's. It was the last available bedroom. She couldn't bring any more girls out until the situation with Cassie was settled. There was no place to put them and there was no way she could afford to put anyone up in a hotel until they found a husband, if Caleb didn't marry them. The way he was behaving it would be months or years before he even considered accepting another woman.

There was a commotion coming from the outside. Maggie could hear yelling coming from the front of the house even though she was in the back showing Cassie her bedroom.

"Excuse me, I'll be right back," she said to Cassie and hurried to the kitchen where the noise was coming from. Once there she heard Fran's mother hollering at someone and him yelling back. Him? Martin! What was he doing here again? Maggie went outside.

"There you are. Will you tell this old biddy to

leave me alone? I came to see you." He held up a bunch of flowers and a box of candy. "I intend to court you."

"Don't talk to Mrs. Lamrona like that and you're being ridiculous. You can't court me. You're a married man. Even if you weren't, I don't want your attentions. Please go away and don't come back."

"You heard her, old man. Don't you speak like that to me. You take your pretty flowers and your candy and go away from here." Maria Lamrona held her ground and didn't let Martin Butler run over the top of her. If Maggie had been matchmaking for him she would have matched him with Maria. They were quite the vocal pair.

"You hush up, woman, and stay out of what is not your business."

Maria stood on the long porch, hands on her hips and yelled at Martin. "It's my business when you continue to insult Mrs. Selby with your advances. She don't want nothing to do with you, you old fool."

It was almost comical to watch. The man up on the horse being chastised like a child by the small woman on the porch. Maggie had to stop herself from laughing out right.

Martin got off his horse and marched up to where Maggie stood on the porch with Maria. "Here." He shoved the flowers and candy at her. She put her arms around her waist and refused to take them. He frowned at her and then shoved them at Maria. "Give these to her later." Then he stomped back to his horse, mounted and galloped out of the yard.

Maria tried to give Maggie the flowers and candy but she shook her head. "You keep them. I don't want anything from that man."

"Good. I like candy," said Maria while she smelled the flowers. She was humming as she went into the house.

*****

Rachel was running and yelling at the same time. "Papa. Papa. You have to come save Maggie from the bad man."

Caleb stopped what he was doing and bent down until he was eye level with his daughter. "What man?"

"I never seen him aftore. He said he was gonna court her but she said no and he got real mad. I'm afraid for her and came to get you."

He'd heard enough. He took off at a run, leaving Rachel to catch up. Rounding the corner of the house he saw Martin Butler gallop away.

He ran to Maggie, who stood on the porch watching Butler. "Are you alright? Rachel was worried he might hurt you."

She shook her head and smiled. "Not as long as Maria is around. You should've seen them. Him, Mr. High and Mighty sitting up on his horse and her giving him what for from the porch. I'm surprised you didn't hear them clear to the barn."

He didn't smile. It wasn't funny. Butler could easily become dangerous. "This has to stop. I'm going to talk to Sheriff Wayburn. Butler can't keep this up. His boldness is escalating and he's scaring my daughter. Eventually he may try something stupid and I really don't want to kill the man."

"You wouldn't." She was aghast.

"If I had to in order to protect you or any member of this household, I wouldn't hesitate."

"Kill him? But he seems harmless enough."

"Now, maybe. But he may not stay that way as he gets more and more frustrated. Sheriff Wayburn needs to be aware. I'll invite him to dinner and we can talk about it. You haven't met him yet and if you're going to set up shop in Golden, you should get to know him."

"I suppose you're right."

"Of course, I am. Besides, he could become one of your clients. He's not married."

"Since I haven't had any responses to my advertisements yet, he could be my first client. Tell me about him."

He shrugged. "Not much to tell. He's a good man. Good at his job. Honest. Hardworking."

"Sounds like a paragon. Does he have any flaws?"

"I doubt he's a paragon of virtue, he is a man

after all, but he has the qualities I require from a man. What a woman requires is an entirely different matter, as you well know."

She nodded in agreement. "Come in and get a cup of coffee. You can tell me more about our good sheriff."

They turned toward the kitchen door and saw Cassie.

Caught, she said to Caleb, "I'm sorry. I really didn't mean to eavesdrop but I couldn't help but overhear about the sheriff. Please tell us more."

Caleb cocked an eyebrow at her.

Cassie shrugged. "Let's face it, Caleb, there's just nothing between us. No offense, Maggie."

"None taken."

"There's more spark between you two than there is Caleb and me. Why don't you take your own advice and get married?" She went to the cupboard, got three cups and poured them each a cup of coffee.

"Yes, Maggie," said Caleb taking the cup from Cassie. "Why don't you take your own advice?"

Maggie wrapped her hands around her cup. When she finally spoke it was in a whisper. "There are many reasons." She looked at Caleb. "Maybe someday I'll be able to explain, but today is not that day. Now, tell us more about the sheriff. What does he look like? Is he tall? Short? Does he have family near?"

Caleb laughed, the mood lightened considerably by Maggie's questions. "Well, let's see. He has light brown hair and I have no idea what color his eyes are, so don't ask. He's a couple of inches shorter than I am but a few pounds heavier and strong as a bull. I know because I wrestled him at last year's Fourth of July celebration. As far as I know, his only relatives are his sister, Ruby, and her husband, Ray. They have a little place north of here. I allow them to run their cattle on part of my range."

"How old is he?" asked Cassie.

Ah, now we're getting to it, he thought. She wants someone younger, not that he blamed her. That was fine with him, he wanted someone older.

Maggie. "He's younger than me. Probably around thirty or so."

Cassie finally smiled. In fact, she looked down right relieved. "I can't wait to meet him."

Caleb almost laughed, but didn't want to embarrass her. "Good. I'll invite him for Sunday dinner. Being a single man, he's always happy for a home cooked meal."

*****

Sunday couldn't arrive soon enough for Cassie. She spent part of every day going over her wardrobe, meager as it was, making sure her Sunday go-to-meeting dress was ironed and ready to put on. Maggie thought she'd seen her iron it on at least two occasions.

When it finally did arrive, she got ready early and spent the rest of the morning pacing in front of the parlor window, watching the road for a sign of horse and rider. After he appeared down the road to the house, she ran back to her room and Maggie was afraid she wasn't going to come out. The girl was having a terrible case of nerves.

"Cassie, come out," Maggie shouted though the closed and locked door.

"No."

"Come on. What's the matter? You've been looking forward to meeting the sheriff for three days."

"What if he doesn't like me?" She opened the door. "What will I do then?"

Maggie walked into the room and took the much taller woman into her arms. "Cassie. Don't worry. I'll find you a husband and you'll stay here until I do. But don't put so much pressure on yourself. You're a lovely girl who also happens to be kind and generous."

"If that's so, why am I twenty-five and not married yet?"

"Because you're looking for the right man, for love and besides," Maggie paused for effect. "The men back in New York are stupid."

Cassie looked at her and burst into laughter. "That's right. I'm going to keep thinking like that. I'm a catch and any man would be lucky to have me. I just need to find the right one for me."

"Okay. Come on now. Let's go and greet the sheriff."

Maggie took Cassie's arm and walked her back to the parlor. Caleb stood there in his Sunday clothes, looking just as good as when she first met him. His dark suit and white shirt emphasized his muscular frame and tan skin. The sun had turned his skin the most delicious caramel, at least to the waist. She'd caught him chopping wood without a shirt and been totally mesmerized. Edgar had never looked like that.

Standing with Caleb was a very handsome man. He had light brown hair as Caleb had said but he didn't mention that it curled just a bit over his collar or that he had piercing caramel colored eyes. Like Caleb, he wore a black suit and tie. He was a little shorter than Caleb and stockier but not fat. All of him looked like muscle. For a fleeting moment, Maggie wondered what a sheriff did to get so muscular.

She looked over at Cassie. The girl was

mesmerized. When she looked back at the sheriff, he seemed to be just as affected by Cassie. Well, how about that? Maggie was making matches and wasn't even trying. Of course, the one match she was trying to make wasn't working out at all. Maybe she was losing her touch.

Caleb cleared his throat. "Robert, may I introduce, Mrs. Maggie Selby and Miss Cassandra Jones."

Robert stepped forward. "Mrs. Selby," he said taking Maggie's outstretched hand.

"Yes. Pleased to make your acquaintance, Sheriff."

"I'm not on duty, please call me Robert."

"Very well, Robert." She moved closer to Cassie, hoping to magically give the girl some support. "This is Cassie."

Robert held out his hand. "You must be Maggie's sister."

Cassis shook her head but her eyes never left his. "No. Actually, we're not related. It just looks that way."

He looked over at Caleb. "How did you get two such lovely women to be staying in your home?"

"Maggie is a matchmaker. She was supposed to be bringing me a bride." Caleb said it with a bit of a smirk, that only Maggie would recognize.

"And Miss Jones?" Robert still hadn't let go of Cassie's hand though Maggie was sure neither of them realized it.

"I…I was…am a client of Maggie's."

"Then there is no one waiting for you back home?"

"No," whispered Cassie.

Caleb cleared his throat and Cassie got her wits about her and extracted her hand from Robert's. Both of them reddened upon realization that they'd been holding hands.

"Let's sit, shall we? I'll see about getting some refreshments. Cassie, would you help me please?" asked Maggie.

"Certainly."

After they were out of the room and out of

earshot, Cassie turned to Maggie, grabbed her by the arm and gushed. "Did you see him? Isn't he the most handsome man you've ever seen?"

"He is attractive," responded Maggie.

"Do you think he likes me?"

"It appeared he was as taken with you as you were with him."

They reached the kitchen and Maggie got four cups out of the cupboard. "Get the coffee pot would you, please?"

Cassie picked up a dishtowel and grabbed the handle of the coffee pot.

When they got back to the parlor, Caleb and Robert were sitting in the arm chairs quietly talking.

"Gentlemen," said Maggie, as she and Cassie entered the room. "Coffee is served." She handed each man a cup and Cassie poured the coffee. Then she and Maggie sat on the sofa with theirs.

"I was just telling Robert about Martin Butler."

"Caleb is definitely right to be concerned. This isn't the first complaint I've had about Butler. He's actually becoming quite the nuisance. Maggie isn't the only woman he's harassing. There was a woman named Beatrice Merryweather that he wouldn't leave alone. She came here as his mail order bride but changed her mind. According to her, he misrepresented himself and she refused to marry him. He refused to take no for an answer and followed her everywhere, demanding she marry him. He began "courting" her. Brought her gifts. That started innocent enough. Flowers, candy, ribbons for her hair. Then he got bolder, giving her lingerie and such. It might not have been so bad but he always made sure to do it in public and embarrassed her greatly. I finally had to put him in jail for a night while Miss Merryweather boarded a train for San Francisco."

"Well, thank the Lord for that. She hadn't written me to tell me what happened. I thought she'd married him and then left. This is much better. At least Beatrice will have the chance for a fresh start."

"She said she had a cousin in San Francisco she could stay with, so I figure she'll be alright," said

Robert.

"That's all well and good for Miss Merryweather," said Caleb. "But how do we keep him from Maggie? I don't want to have to kill him, Robert, but I will if I have to."

"I'll have a talk with him. Get him to see things from the perspective of the law. You do what you need to do in order to keep your family safe."

Caleb nodded.

Maggie didn't like where the conversation had gone. As much as she disliked Martin Butler she felt he was harmless and surely didn't want him dead.

"Well, now that's solved. I believe Fran has dinner ready for us in the dining room. Shall we?"

Caleb took Maggie's arm and escorted her while Robert did the same with Cassie.

Rachel, Fran, Maria and Tom joined them in the dining room, while the cowboys ate in the kitchen. Even if they'd wanted to eat with the men, there wasn't room. The table simply wouldn't hold them all. In this case, Maggie wanted their meal to be a little more formal since they had a guest. She wouldn't have sat in the kitchen even if it had held them all.

She sat Cassie next to Robert with Caleb at the head of the table and Rachel on his left. Maggie put herself on Caleb's right followed by Maria, Fran and then Tom at the other end of the table. It didn't occur to her until they sat to eat that she'd put couples together, including her and Caleb. Why had she done that? She had to get out of here. She was too close and getting closer by the day.

"Maggie. Maggie!" Caleb snapped his fingers.

She blinked and shook her head bringing her back to the present. "I'm sorry. What were you saying?"

"It doesn't matter. What were you thinking? You were far away from here."

"Nothing really. We can talk later."

He cocked his head to one side, his eyes narrowed in question, but he let it go. "Alright. But know this. I won't forget and we will talk."

She gave him a curt nod.

"Papa. May I be excused?" Rachel had finished her dinner and was ready to go play.

"Yes, but go put on your play clothes before you go outside." He looked down his nose at her. "Promise."

She crossed her heart and said, "Yes, Papa. I promise."

"Alright. Skedaddle." He swatted her little bottom as she turned and ran from the room.

"She's turning into quite the little lady. Ruth would be proud," said Robert.

"Thanks. She can still be a little hellion when she's a mind to," smiled Caleb. "Reminds me of her mother."

It was like a cold bucket of water hit her square in the face. Caleb still loved his wife. Even if she changed her mind about marrying again, he wouldn't love her. The realization that she even contemplated marriage surprised and scared her. Now that Fran was here to cook and Maria did most of the cleaning and the laundry, there wasn't really a reason for Maggie to stay. Except one. A big one. She'd given her word and her word was her bond. She couldn't back out.

She put her fork down. For some reason her appetite was gone.

CHAPTER 5

Caleb didn't forget. He wanted to talk to Maggie almost as soon as the sheriff had left. Luckily for her so did Cassie and she didn't wait to get Maggie alone.

"Maggie, I think Robert liked me. He asked if he could call on me and I told him, 'yes'. Is that alright?"

"Of course. I'm glad for you."

"You aren't mad that I won't be marrying Caleb?" Cassie whispered. She looked warily at Caleb who was chomping at the bit waiting to talk to Maggie.

"Goodness, no. I want my ladies to be happy.

Anyone could see that you and Caleb aren't right for each other."

Maggie locked arms with her. "Come to the parlor and tell me everything you talked about."

Caleb frowned and gave her an 'I'll get you later' look but didn't say anything. Instead he went to his bedroom and changed into his work clothes. He stopped by the parlor on the way outside. "If you want me I'll be out at the corral. We're breaking some new horses. You might find it interesting if you'd like to come and watch."

"We just might do that," said Maggie. "It would be good to get outside on such a fine day." Actually, she was kind of excited to watch Caleb work. Seeing his muscles move and flex gave her shivers and heated her in all the right places.

"Later, then." He said it pointedly. Maggie knew he wasn't talking about the horses or corral. He meant to talk about what was troubling her. She'd gotten a small reprieve, that's all. What was bothering her was the thought of bringing another girl out as a bride for him. She didn't want to talk to him about that. The ugly truth was she didn't want to find a bride. Perhaps it would be best to simply stop trying. She thought of the other brides he'd turned down and was nearly struck dumb by what she'd done. With the exception of Cassie, whom she really thought he'd like, she'd sent him candidates she knew he'd reject. They were not what he was asking for at all. She knew then that she'd fallen in love with Caleb Black. Consciously or not, she'd been sabotaging her own efforts to find him a bride. She wanted him for herself, except it scared her silly. How could she want a man when the one she'd had treated her so badly? What was the matter with her?

She had to admit it. She was wrong, and needed to get out of the way for his happiness. She'd have Sally choose some candidates based on the criteria that Caleb had put in his original letter. Before he'd known Maggie, before they'd corresponded with each other, before she'd fallen in love with the funny, witty, gentle yet strong man in his letters.

Since they'd met she'd only fallen deeper. The only thing keeping her away from him was fear that he could turn into Edgar. Irrational or not, the fear was real. Even though she knew in her heart that wasn't possible. There was no way he could be like Edgar and love Rachel as he did. He was such a good father. He deserved to have more children. He wanted more children and she couldn't give those to him, even if she'd been foolish enough to change her mind and marry him. It wouldn't be fair to him.

She'd tell him she was leaving tomorrow. Fran could make them a nice picnic and he'd take her to the summer pasture he'd wanted to show her. Though she suspected it was only so he could get her alone. Perhaps that's what she wanted, too. Would it really be so bad to take some memories to warm the cold, lonely nights ahead?

If she slept with him would he think he'd won? Would he think her wanton? Was she? Would he believe that she would marry him now that they'd made love? She had to be completely open and above board, make him understand it would make no difference. It was just...he made her feel what she'd never felt before. Desire. Her heart thundered every time he was near. When he touched her, it skipped a beat and as much as she tried not to, she always sounded breathless when he was close and they were alone.

Even after all these weeks, she still felt the same. And it scared her to death.

*****

Later that afternoon, she and Cassie went down to the corrals. Caleb was mounting one of the new horses. This one had a red coat on its front half and was mostly white with spots on it on its rear end. An appaloosa he'd called it. He had several in the small herd of horses he kept.

Almost as soon as he sat on the saddle, the horse started bucking, trying to dislodge the load from his back. It kicked out its back legs and threw its back up and forward. Caleb hung on with his legs, every muscle outlined beneath snug denim pants and by a rope around the animals middle that he'd wound his hand into. Muscles along his back flexed with each kick of the horse. Sweat dampened his shirt and Maggie held her breath during the terrifying and blessedly short spectacle.

It seemed like hours yet it was only seconds before the animal quieted and Caleb cantered around the perimeter of the corral several times to make sure the horse was broke to the saddle.

Maggie had never seen anything so spectacular as watching him tame the horse.

He rode over to where she and Cassie stood, their arms draped over the top rail of the corral. One of the cowboys ran up and took the horse by the bridle while Caleb dismounted.

"Well, what did you ladies think?"

"Very exciting," said Cassie.

"Very frightening," said Maggie. "What if you'd gotten thrown off? You could have been trampled or broken your neck and died."

Caleb took off his gloves and swatted them back and forth across his thigh. Clouds of dust rose with each swat.

He broke into a big grin. "Were you worried about me?"

She raised her chin a notch. "No more than I would have been for any other cowboy. It's dangerous."

He shrugged. "It's part of running a ranch. There are a lot of things about this life that are dangerous. It's why we try to live our lives to the fullest. Grabbing for what joy we can whenever it comes our way." He ran a single finger along her jaw. "You're my joy, Maggie," he whispered for her ears alone.

*****

Cassie and Maggie sat in the parlor as they did every night after supper. Maggie with her needlepoint and Cassie knitting. Caleb took Rachel to bed to read her a story but would return shortly.

"Cassie, I want you to go to bed earlier tonight than usual. I need to speak to Caleb privately."

"Sure. I can leave now if you'd like. I got a new book when we were in Golden last Saturday and I've been dying to start it."

"No need to hurry. How is it going with you and Robert? I know he's been out to the ranch at least three times in the last two weeks."

Cassie's cheeks turned pink. "We can't see each other as often as we'd like, but we're doing the best we can. I think he's going to ask me to marry him."

Maggie put down the needlepoint she was working on. "Wow. That's fast."

Cassie shrugged. "Not as fast as it would have been had I been a mail order bride for him. We're actually getting to know each other first."

"I'm not criticizing," said Maggie, looking up from her needlepoint. "I'm very glad you two found each other."

"What about you and Caleb?"

"Ouch." She poked herself with her needle. "There is no me and Caleb."

"Only in your mind," smiled Cassie.

"What's only in her mind?" asked Caleb when he walked in.

"Nothing. I just poked my finger." She looked

up from her needlepoint, the injured finger in her mouth. "Did you get Rachel down?"

He chuckled. "She was out before the Mad Hatter's tea party ended."

"I'm so glad she's enjoying the book. I would have liked it when I was a girl."

He sat in the chair next to her in front of the fire and across from the settee where Cassie sat. Smiling, he said, "I can picture you as a girl. Bright red pigtails bouncing in the sunshine, the cutest freckles across your nose, just like now and the devil in your green eyes. Just like now."

"I'll have you know there was never the devil in my eyes. I was the perfect child."

Caleb let out a shout of laughter.

Maggie laughed, too, remembering the hell she'd put her parents through, when she wasn't working in the fields, that is. Her curiosity often got the best of her and got her in a lot of trouble. Much as it had now.

Cassie rose. "I think I'm going to retire a little early tonight. I have a new book I'm dying to start reading."

"Have a good night," said Maggie, giving her a hug. "Thank you," she whispered in her ear.

Caleb also rose and stood by his chair. "Sleep well."

After Cassie left Caleb turned to Maggie. "Well, you have me all to yourself. What shall we do?" He waggled his eyebrows at her and winked.

"Stop that," she said returning to her chair and the basket of needlepoint in the seat. She picked up the basket and put it on the floor then sat down with her hands folded demurely in her lap. "I wanted to talk to you. Actually, I wanted to ask if you'd like to go on a picnic with me."

Caleb cocked an eyebrow. You want to go on a picnic with me? What's that catch?"

"Why does there have to be a catch?"

"Because I know you. But," he shrugged, "very well, you want to go on a picnic."

"Yes."

"Will Cassie be coming?"

"No."

He leaned back in his chair and stretched his long legs out in front of him towards the fire. "Just the two of us?"

She nodded. "Yes. I thought you could show me the summer pasture. You've been wanting to."

"And you haven't wanted to go. Aren't you afraid to be alone with me? I might take advantage of your girlish sensibilities."

She looked into his eyes. So vulnerable despite the bravado. "No. I'm not afraid to be alone with you. I was never worried about you and what you might do but about me. I just want to see some of the countryside and the weather has been so beautiful."

He leaned toward her. "I'd love to take you on a picnic."

"Good. Can we go tomorrow?"

"I can't. I still have a few horses to break. How about the next day?" He got up and went to the fireplace, putting it at his back so he could face her.

"That would be wonderful. I'll have Fran make

us a nice lunch. We *will* be able to take the buggy won't we? I don't think I'm up for riding in the saddle all that way."

"Probably not all the way to the summer pasture, but I have a pretty spot to take you to. You'll like it. I promise."

She smiled at him. "Thank you. I'm looking forward to it." She rose to go to her room.

Caleb grabbed her hand, raised it to his lips and said, "No. Thank you. I'll see you to your room."

She started to protest but decided she'd like for him to see her to her room. To walk with her. Now was the time to begin enjoying her life. It was much too short to live by the strictures of the Eastern society she no longer belonged to. She wouldn't be here for very much longer and wanted to pack as many memories as she could in the time she had left. She may hurt him but she couldn't help that. As much as she wanted to stay, her fear was too great. Too great to keep her from leaving.

He held the door for her. "I won't bite."

She preceded him out of the room and down

the hall. "I never thought you would," she said over her shoulder.

"Unless you want me to," he said softly.

She stopped, surprised by his words. "Caleb," she admonished him.

He laughed, clearly tickled to get a rise out of her.

"Are you going to make me regret my decision to go alone with you?"

They'd reached her room.

He placed his hand on her shoulder and turned her to face him. "Maggie. I don't want you to ever regret being with me."

Taking her face between his palms he lowered his head. His lips, soft upon hers as he kissed her. Her insides turned to mush and she only wanted to get closer to him. Her arms wrapped around his neck as his arms came around her and held her close. He deepened the kiss and she was lost. All she could do, all she wanted to do, was return his kiss, feel it, savor it. Make a memory.

When they broke apart they both were

breathless.

"Don't tell me we shouldn't be doing that," said Caleb, resting his forehead against hers. "It's too good. Ah, Maggie, we're good. Together. Can't you see that?"

She looked up into those beautiful brandy eyes. It was so hard to remain strong. "I won't marry. I can't. Can't you understand? I know you're not Edgar and never will be but I can't, I won't allow anyone to have that kind of dominance over me. In marriage, I have no more rights than your cattle, you'd own me. I've worked too hard to be independent, to be free, to give it all up."

"I'm not asking you to. You can continue with your business."

"You see? That's the point," she stepped away out of his arms. "I have to have your permission if we get married. I don't need anyone's permission to do anything within the law. Someday I hope all women will have the same rights as men but today is not that day."

He took a deep breath and then sighed. "You

have valid concerns. I understand your fears. I hope someday to alleviate them."

She opened the door to her room. "I'm not sure that's possible. But thank you anyway. Good night."

He stepped away from the door farther into the hall. "Good night."

*****

The day of their picnic dawned bright with cobalt blue skies and sunshine. Fran fixed them a picnic of fried chicken, potato salad, cheese, apples and a bottle of sweet cider. Maggie packed a quilt for them to lay on the ground.

Caleb was all smiles as he climbed down from the buggy to help her up.

"Let me assist you," he said in his best knightly voice and with a deep bow. He'd been doing the voice and many others, as he read to Rachel from Alice's Adventures in Wonderland. The 1865 novel was still one of Maggie's favorites.

She could play along. "Thank you, kind sir," she said with a curtsy and a giggle.

Caleb got in and flicked the reins down on the horses behinds. They started walking. He slapped them again and they began to trot. He headed west from the ranch on a road that was little more than two rutted tracks.

They reached the foothills and the road started to climb and wind its way up the hill. About half way up the hill, Caleb turned off onto a trail which he followed up and over a rise. They descended down into a small valley. A stream ran through the middle and fed into a small pond. It was as green and lush as anything she'd seen back East. There was a little cabin atop a little rise near to the pond. Scent from the Ponderosa pines filled the air. Aspen trees dotted the valley floor, their leaves shimmering in the gentle breeze.

"It's beautiful. Is it yours?"

"Yes. Ruth and I stumbled upon it when we were first married. I had to buy it. It belonged to an old miner who was pulling up stakes and happy to be rid of it."

"Oh," she said looking away and out into the

valley.

"Why do you do that?"

"Do what?"

"Get a sad look and turn away whenever I mention Ruth?"

"I didn't realize I did," she said, still not looking at him afraid he'd see the unshed tears in her eyes. As much as she didn't want to marry, she wanted to believe that he was capable of loving her. Not likely, if he was still in love with his wife.

"Maggie, look at me."

She shook her head.

He placed a finger on her chin and gently turned her toward him. "I can't pretend that Ruth didn't exist. She gave me the most precious of gifts. Rachel. I will be forever grateful to her for that."

"You still love her."

He was silent for a few moments. "I cared for her. Ruth and I grew up together. We always assumed we'd marry so when she turned twenty-two we did. I'd sowed my wild oats by that time. I was twenty-four and had been on my own for a long time. I'd started the ranch and was doing well at it. We were married for eight years before she got pregnant with Rachel. The pregnancy wasn't easy for her. The doctor was sure she'd lose the baby before she could bring it to full term. Ruth was determined that wouldn't happen. She stayed in bed for most of the last three months. Anything she could do to keep that baby. Turned out she was right and gave birth to Rachel. But it took everything out of her and it was too much for her fragile body to withstand.

"She was a lot like you. Independent and stubborn to the core. She didn't have the red hair that you do but she might as well have. Let's get down and walk a bit."

Maggie let him help her down then he held his arm out for her. She took it and he placed his free hand on top of hers. She was sorry that Ruth had died and yet not. If she hadn't died, she wouldn't have met Caleb. But she hated to see Caleb and Rachel so sad.

"The cabin?" she nodded toward the small structure at the other end of the pond. "You built it?"

"Yes, but not for the reason you think. It wasn't for us. It's a line shack for my men. Someplace they can go and be safe from the weather if they need to be. It's stocked with firewood, tinned food, bed, blankets, there should even be a deck of cards."

"It's good of you to think of something like that."

"I have several around my property. Sometimes in Colorado, the weather can change in an instant and there isn't enough time to get back to the ranch to get out of it."

They were silent for a while, just walking together. Taking in the sights, sounds and smells of the glorious countryside. Maggie was still in awe of the beauty she saw everyday. Flowers of every color imaginable surrounded them. Purple columbines, red Indian paintbrushes, white honeysuckle and blue bluebells, plus many more she couldn't name yet. There was that word. Yet. If she stayed. But she couldn't. It was getting too hard to resist him. He was nothing if not persistent.

He'd given cursory attention to Cassie when she arrived, but that was all. He was polite, nothing more. There had been no spark. Not like between him and Maggie. If only she could surrender to her feelings. But then that was the problem. Surrender. She couldn't give up all that she'd worked so hard to get for the unknown. Caleb, as wonderful as he was, was still the unknown.

Then stay, her mind told her. *Find out what he is, who he is. Make him the known rather than the unknown. I can't. What if he finds me lacking, like Edgar did? He's not Edgar*, her mind said. He's Caleb and he's a good man. *Yes, one who deserves much better than me.*

"You're awfully quiet."

"I was just thinking how beautiful it is here. Thank you for bringing me."

He rubbed her hand. "You're welcome. I'm glad you like it. The only problem is that it's starting to rain and if rains hard we could get caught in a flash flood. We have to get to the shack quick and get the horse into the shelter there. I built it on the high ground for just such an occasion. That's why it's not closer to the pond and the stream."

Caleb whipped the horses into a gallop and as the buggy rocked back and forth, Maggie held on for dear life to the strap hooked to the side wall next to her. Caleb seemed unaffected by the jostling, his concentration focused solely on getting them to safety before a flash flood.

They reached the cabin in time, though soaked clean through. The quilt was dry as Maggie had put it inside the buggy under the seat.

Caleb came around to help her. She retrieved the basket and the blanket and followed him inside the small shack. It was cold. Her soaking clothes did nothing to ward off the chill.

He went to the wood pile next to the fireplace and quickly started a fire.

"I have to take care of the horses. I'll be right back."

Maggie nodded not trusting her teeth not to chatter if she tried to speak. While he was gone she explored the cabin. Had to keep moving to stay warm. There was a bed along one wall with sheets and blankets neatly folded on top of it. Across the room from the bed was a table with two chairs. On the wall between the table and the bed was the fireplace, opposite that was the door. The cabin was small and functional but nothing more. Just enough for a cowboy for a night or two.

When Caleb returned she was standing in front of the fire holding her hands out to it. She was still freezing.

He came up behind her and rubbed her arms up and down vigorously.

"Maggie, you're freezing. We need to get out of these wet clothes."

She shook her head. "I'm fine. I'll be fine." Her teeth chattered with each word and she was sure she was turning blue.

"You're being obstinate. If you don't get out of those wet clothes you'll take a chill. Now are you going to do it yourself or do I have to take them off for you?"

When she didn't move, he started to unbutton her dress. She swatted his hands away. "I'll do it. Give me the quilt out of the basket and turn around."

He dutifully handed her the quilt. "Sure you don't need help with those buttons? Your hands are shaking, they're so cold."

"I'll be fine. Turn around."

Sighing, he turned his back on her. She could see he was undoing his own buttons and soon his shirt came off. Her hands stilled and she squeaked. Caleb quickly twisted around. Faced with all that naked chest she could only stare. Edgar had never looked like this.

"Are you all right?" he asked, stepping closer.

She nodded. "I...I'm...good."

"You're not good. Hurry up and get out of those wet things."

He turned his back on her again and she hurried with her clothes. Her dress pooled on the floor in a sodden mess followed by her chemise and bloomers. She took off her shoes and socks which were also soaked. Totally naked, she was almost shivering too much to wrap the quilt around her. Immediately the dry cloth started warming her up.

"You can look now."

Caleb turned and his eyes widened. "You're beautiful."

"I'm in a quilt."

"Yes, but it does nothing to hide your beauty."

"You're going to freeze if you don't get out of those pants. Do what I did and wrap yourself in the blanket from the bed." She didn't wait to see if he did it, instead she started laying out her clothes on the floor in front of the fire.

"All done. You can look now."

He had wrapped the blanket around his waist leaving his chest gloriously naked. She almost swallowed her tongue. She couldn't take her eyes off of him.

"You're staring."

She closed her mouth and her eyes. "Sorry.

It's just...well...Edgar never looked like you do."

"I'll take that as a compliment."

"Oh, yes." She opened her eyes and nodded her head vigorously. "Most definitely a compliment."

He chuckled. "I'm glad you like what you see."

Maggie faced away from him unable to look and not stare. Unfortunately, where she faced was toward the bed. Oh dear.

"Maggie."

"What?"

"Sit at the table and I'll make us some coffee. There's a barrel to catch rain water just outside the door and coffee on the shelf. Why don't you get that deck of cards and we'll play poker."

"I don't know how to play poker."

"Good. I'll teach you." Under his breath he added, "it'll keep us both busy."

She went to the shelf on the wall next to the fireplace and grabbed the single deck of cards. Then she went to the fire and took down her hair. It would never dry wrapped in the bun. Moving her dress she sat on the floor in front of the fire and undid the bun, running her fingers through her hair.

She heard a sharp intake of breath and looked up to see Caleb watching her, coffeepot in hand.

"Are you all right?" she asked him, getting up from the floor and going to him. When he didn't say anything she said, "Caleb?"

"I've never seen you with your hair down. It's beautiful."

She lowered her eyes and took a fistful of her hair. "I thought about cutting it off so many times but just couldn't. It's one of the few things I've always been proud of."

He came closer, reached out and took some into his hand. "It's so soft. Just like silk."

"Thank you."

Winding her hair in his hand he brought her closer. "Maggie," he said as his lips crashed down on hers. He drank from her, taking and giving. His tongue clashed with hers dueling, playing.

Maggie wrapped her arms around his neck and

held him to her. Sharing, taking all he had to give. She wanted this more than anything. Wanted this memory.

"Caleb."

"Let me love you."

"Yes." Her quilt had worked its way loose without her arms to hold it up. She released it completely, letting it fall to the floor.

"God, you're beautiful." He let his own blanket join hers then picked her up and carried her to the bed. He let her slide down his fully aroused body as he set her on her feet. That was another part of him that was totally unlike Edgar. He'd been poorly endowed compared to Caleb who was long and thick. So much so she was a little intimidated.

"Caleb, I don't know about this. You're so much...*more* than Edgar was. What if you don't fit?"

His head fell back and he whooped with laughter.

She tried to pull away. "Don't laugh at me."

He held her fast. "I'm not laughing at you but at your naiveté. Edgar was an idiot and it turns out he was not a well-formed idiot. Trust me. We are going to be beautiful together."

"I'm glad, because so far this feels really good." And it did. His chest was lightly covered with soft hair that tickled her nipples making them erect. She rubbed back and forth, loving the sensation.

"I would guess from your actions that Edgar had no chest hair either."

"No, he didn't. Looking at your body gives me great pleasure. I never felt pleasure of any kind with him. Only pain." She looked away, not wanting him to see the guilt in her eyes. She was lacking, Edgar always made sure she knew that. Caleb was so handsome, she couldn't imagine what he wanted with someone like her.

He nudged her chin with his finger. "Look at me."

She turned and looked up at him. His eyes held no contempt, no criticism, only compassion, caring.

"You will never know pain again. I will always give you pleasure. Always."

"I've never had pleasure coupling," she admitted.

"Then let's start your instruction."

"I'd like that." She wrapped her arms around his neck again. "I'd like that very much." Taking the lead, filled with new confidence from his words, she pressed her lips to his and then ran her tongue along the seam of his lips until he opened for her. She plunged into his mouth and plundered and he let her. He helped her, twining his tongue with hers. Then he pulled back and kissed her gently, softly. He moved up and down her neck, his whiskers tickling as he kissed her senseless.

Each move he made stoked her. Each kiss warmed her and she melted at his touch.

"Make love to me. Now."

"My pleasure." He leaned her back on the bed and came down over her, bracing his weight on his elbows to keep from crushing her.

She closed her eyes out of habit. It was the

only way she could endure Edgar's groping.

"Maggie. Keep your eyes open. I want to see you. I want you to see me, not Edgar."

She opened her eyes and looked up at him. "I'm sorry. It's an old habit."

"Never again. Remember?"

She nodded.

He kissed her lips, then her neck and the little hollow between her collar bones. Moving down her body, he kissed the tops of her breasts and then licked her in a single swipe down to her nipple which he sucked into his mouth.

She cried out at the sensations and arched her back holding his head to her. "Oh, God!"

Caleb lifted his head releasing her nipple. "Like that, do you?"

"Yes," she answered, out of breath.

"Then you're going to love what's coming up." He bent his head and took her other nipple into his mouth while he rolled the first one between his fingers.

The pleasure traveled directly from her nipples

to her core and she felt moisture between her legs.

Caleb kissed his way down her belly until he was there. At the junction of her thighs. At her private parts that ached for him. He stopped, looked up at her and grinned wickedly before plunging his face into her. He parted her nether lips with his fingers and found a place that sent her up and off the bed.

She'd never felt anything as amazing as what he was doing to her. An ache built in her, deep inside, building, building to something she wanted but was just out of her reach. "Caleb. Help me."

He slid one finger, then two inside her. He scissored them up and down, then pulled them forward until he touched her on that spot that sent her flying. She bucked him, and yet held him, then she soared among the stars and called his name.

Licking her, softly, he removed his fingers but stayed with her until she quieted. She panted, her breasts heaving like she'd been working hard. Her legs relaxed next to his body.

"*That* was amazing."

He chuckled. "Now we're going to do it again."

She shook her head. "I don't think I can survive it again."

He worked his way up her body, kissing her until he reached her mouth. "Sure you can. You'll see."

She kissed him back amazed to find that the fires inside her were building again with each kiss he gave her. Grabbing his head, she kissed him fully.

He pulled back and positioned himself at her entrance. "You're prepared for me. Now see how well we fit." With those words he pushed into her. She was slick and wet, ready for him. It had been a long time since she'd had sex, so she was tight, almost like she was a virgin again. Caleb took it slow. Let her get used to him. Let her stretch.

Sweat beaded on his brow. She knew he was going slow for her but she didn't want slow. She wanted him in her, all the way now. Lifting herself she forced him further in.

"Maggie, stop. I don't want to hurt you."

"You're not hurting me. Come into me. All the way."

"If you're sure," he said as he pulled out and then slammed into her sliding all the way home.

"Yes, that's wonderful,"

He began to move within her, slowly out almost all the way and then in, he built it, stoked her passion.

"Touch yourself," he commanded.

"Me? I've never...,"

"Watch me, feel me," he balanced himself on one arm and touched her with his fingers, rubbing that special spot she'd felt before. He stopped and put his weight on both arms. "Now you do it."

She reached down and felt herself, found the little nub that he'd been rubbing and circled her finger around it. "Oh my!"

He chuckled. "Like it?"

"Yes, it's almost as good as when you did it."

"Keep it up, sweetheart, we're going on a ride now."

He began to pump into her hard, touching her womb with each inward thrust while she rubbed her bud. The fire in her built to an inferno. The volcano she'd become was about to burst.

"Caleb," she cried out.

"Now, sweet, now." He stroked in hard, once, twice and then he shouted her name. She followed in short order, reaching the stars at the same time he did.

He collapsed on her, his breathing ragged. Hers was no better. She loved the feel of his weight on her. She wrapped her arms around him but her legs were lank at his side. She was spent. Two times. She'd had two amazing orgasms. Never in her life had she felt so alive and so exhausted.

Lifting himself off her, he rolled away and took her with him, tucking her into his side. She couldn't help but notice that she fit perfectly like they *were* made for each other.

"Thank you."

"No, thank you. That was incredible. Do you still think we won't fit together?"

"Oh, no. We are perfect," she said before she caught herself.

"That's what I've been trying to tell you. We are perfect. Marry me, Maggie."

"I told you I can't. That hasn't changed just because we had sex." She tried to pull away from him.

"No you don't. I like you just where you are. I'm going to take advantage of you at every opportunity, hoping you'll change your mind."

"I won't, but you can try. As a matter of fact, I like it when you take advantage of me. Please continue, to at your leisure." She kissed his chest and forgot the reasons she told herself she couldn't do this. It was wonderful and she would think of these times when she was back in New York.

Alone.

CHAPTER 6

They spent two nights at the cabin. It rained sheets all the first night and the road was too muddy to get up with the buggy the next day. She knew everyone would be worried about them. She was most concerned with Rachel. The sweet girl would be beside herself worrying about her papa.

Caleb kept her occupied making love and playing cards. Their clothes finally dried out but they didn't put them on until they were getting ready to leave. Maggie found that it was quite freeing to go around naked for a couple of days. If it were just she and Caleb she might never wear clothes again. At least she'd never want him to wear them. His body was delightful to look at. All strong planes and lean lines, muscular without being bulky. Perfect as far as she was concerned. And the things he could do with that body, the things he had her doing. Just the thought made heat rush to her core.

"There you go again. Thinking about what we've done here the last two days," he teased.

"How do you know what I'm thinking?"

"You blush, from your breasts to the top of your head. It's quite lovely really, because I know that I'm the cause of that blush. And I'll always know. When we get back home, I'll know every time you think about us." He took her in his arms, their clothes seeming to be such an encumbrance now. "I love that you think about us. That I can make you blush and that you smile at the same time. I'm going to miss this, miss our private time together."

She wrapped her arms around him and laid her head on his chest. Unwilling to let reality intrude just yet. "You're just saying that because I beat you at poker."

"I let you win."

"You didn't!"

"Alright, I didn't. You caught on very quickly. Want to play one last game? We could bet our clothes. I know both of us will be the winner that way."

She shook her head and stood away from him, already bereaved at the loss of his body from hers. She'd never get enough of him. Not if they had all the time in the world, which they didn't.

"We need to get home. Rachel has got to be worried about her papa who hasn't been home to read to her for two nights. Fran and Tom have probably got a search party out looking for us. No, we need to go back." Back to reality, bleak reality.

Caleb nodded. "I suppose you're right." He looked around the shack. "Doesn't look like we were ever here."

They were mostly quiet on the ride back to the ranch. There wasn't much to say. Caleb had tried to change her mind again and again, even going so far as to try withholding her orgasm. Nothing had worked. She was adamant. She wouldn't give up her freedom and there was no reason for them to marry. They were good together in bed, but it wasn't as if they loved each other. When she'd asked him if he loved her, he remained silent for a moment and then answered that he 'cared' for her.

"Maggie, I don't know that I can love anyone like you want to be loved. Like you need to be loved. I don't know if I have it in me."

"What about Ruth?"

"I told you I cared for her, but I don't believe that I ever loved her. At least not the way you mean. We were great friends. You and I could be that too, if you'd let us."

"I want more than that. I want someone who loves me to distraction."

"I know you do and I don't deny you deserve it."

"But you want me to settle for less? Less than what I deserve? Less than what I need? I had a loveless marriage. I won't have another one." She looked at the countryside as they passed. He didn't dispute it or try anymore to change her mind.

In a few hours the ranch came into view. Two men on horseback came charging up the hill toward them.

"Hiya, Boss," said one of the cowboys. "Tom was just sendin' us up to check the western line shack. We done checked everywhere else we could think of to find you. What happened anyway?"

"We got caught in a thunderstorm and couldn't get the buggy out of the valley until it dried up some. Nothin' to worry about."

"Good to have ya back. We'll let Tom know." The cowboys galloped away back toward the ranch.

They were still thirty minutes away from home. It was now or never. She had to tell him her decision.

"Caleb. I…I've come to a decision."

"Sounds like I'm not going to like it, so spit it out."

"I'm going to go back to New York." She clasped her hands in her lap so they wouldn't shake.

"I'm not doing any good staying here. For either of us."

He slowed the team and turned toward her. "So it's easier to run away than face the fact that we were made to be together?"

She heard the anger and the hurt in his voice. Did he perhaps care for her more than he admitted? It didn't matter it wasn't enough. She wanted all or nothing.

"Yes. It's easier than staying here and having to face you everyday knowing you can never love me." She loved him. It took all she had in her to remain strong and not settle for just his caring. She wanted so much more from him.

He nodded and turned back to the horses. He flicked the reins and got them moving at a good pace again. "When will you go?"

"I want to see Cassie and Robert married. It should be soon. Do you mind if I stay a little longer? I can leave right away if you'd rather."

"Stay as long as you like." His voice was flat. He was hurting. She knew that and would take it all back if there was even an inkling that he could love her more than just physically.

The last two days were magical.

"I wish we didn't have to return to reality. I wish so many things."

"So do I, Maggie. So do I."

He kept his focus on the horses while she looked down at her hands, willing the tears in her eyes not to fall. It would do no good for him to know how much this affected her.

When they arrived back at the house, Caleb came around and helped her down, just as he always did. But this time, his hands didn't linger, his gaze was distant and he couldn't wait to get away from her.

"I'll take the basket to the kitchen," said Maggie. "So you can see to the horses."

He nodded and got back into the buggy.

She didn't blame him. What was there to say? How in the world was she going to stand this for another two or three weeks?

Rachel came running out of the house and

threw herself at Maggie. "I was so worried when you and Papa didn't come home. Why didn't you come home?"

Maggie bent down and gave her a hug. "We got stuck in the rain. Then the road was so muddy we couldn't get the buggy up the hill to get out of the valley. We would have come home if we could have. Your papa would never have you worry about him."

"I know. I figured it was something like that but when you didn't come home last night neither, I got worried."

"I'm sorry, sweetie. If we could have been home sooner< we would have."

Rachel hugged her. "I'm just glad you're here now. It's all better."

Maggie closed her eyes and hugged the child to her. *If only you knew how much better it's not. How am I going to say goodbye to you? I love you so much.*

She and Rachel walked hand in hand to the kitchen. Cassie and Fran were both there and started talking at once.

Holding up her hands, Maggie said, "Ladies. Ladies. Please. One at a time."

Cassie and Fran looked at each other and then Cassie said, "Where have you been? We've been worried sick. Afraid that some accident befell you and Caleb."

Maggie explained for what seemed like the umpteenth time what happened. Cassie and Fran looked at each other again and smiled.

"So...," said Fran.

"So what?" answered Maggie.

"So what happened?"

"Nothing. We played cards." And made love. At least for her it was love. He made such sweet, passionate love to her. It was nothing like Edgar who had looked upon it as his duty, not his pleasure. But Caleb derived only pleasure from it and gave her only pleasure back. That couldn't happen if he didn't love her, right?

She had a few weeks to change his mind. Could she?

"Now, Cassie, tell me what's happening with you and Robert. Did he propose?"

"He did. Last night." She held up her hand and there was a ring with a small diamond in it. "Isn't it lovely? It was his mothers."

"It's beautiful," said Maggie, taking the younger woman in her arms. "I'm so happy for you. What about you Fran? Have you and Tom set a date yet?"

"Actually we have. Cassie, Robert, Tom and I decided to make it a double wedding. Then we only have to have one party. Since it would be all the same people, it makes financial sense to do it this way."

"Wonderful. When is the day?"

"Two weeks from Sunday," said Fran.

"Oh my, there's so much to do. We have to get dresses and arrange food," said Maggie.

"We've already been talking about it. Since I sew better than Fran, I'm making the dresses and Fran is going to do all the cooking with the help of Maria."

"And me?" asked Maggie.

"You get to do the decorating. We thought that Rachel could help," said Cassie, smiling down at Rachel.

"I'm good at decoratin'. What's decoratin'?" she asked looking up at Maggie.

All three women laughed.

*****

Maggie was afraid Caleb might never talk to her again. The only time he did was to grunt one word answers usually 'no'.

She was almost done milking the cow, having given Rachel the day off, when he came into the barn. She didn't even look up, no need since he wouldn't talk to her anyway.

Suddenly he was behind her, rubbing her back and neck like he used to. Her head dropped back and all the memories she held inside came flooding back.

"Caleb," she whispered.

"Maggie. I've missed you."

"And I you."

"Come with me." He helped her stand.

"Where are we going?"

"To the hay loft. For some privacy."

She nodded and let him lead the way.

Once they were in the loft, he stopped and turned to her. "Are you sure? Don't tease me about this, Maggie." He gathered her in his arms. "I want this more than almost anything."

She wrapped her arms around his neck. "I'm not teasing. I want this, too. For as long as I'm here, I want you to make love to me. Just don't think that this will get me to stay. I'm still leaving."

He pulled her close again. "I agree," he whispered into her hair.

She knew he'd use this as a way to get her to stay. She wasn't so naïve as to believe he'd change his mind so easily, but she was as determined as he was. Then he closed his lips over hers and she lost all train of thought. Everything in her focused on his lips and hers. Meeting, clashing, feasting.

Caleb moved his hands up and cradled her face, tracing her cheeks with his thumbs, sending lightning bolts shooting through her. It seemed forever since she felt this close to him even though it had only been days. No one had ever held her with such gentleness or gave her so much joy as Caleb did just with his kiss. Maggie melted. She leaned into him, returning his passion with her own.

He moved his hands down her neck, gently caressing as he went. She felt her pulse pound beneath his finger tips. He swept over the buttons on her dress, untied the laces on her chemise until she was bared to the waist.

"Lovely as I remembered, as I've been dreaming about. You haunt me in my dreams," he said as he cupped the soft globes. He grazed his thumbs over her nipples, his calluses abrading them until they were turgid little peaks.

Her head fell back and the only thing keeping her upright was her grip on his shoulders.

"Oh, Caleb. That feels so good. It's been too long. Don't make me wait."

"Darlin' you're going to wait and then you're going to scream my name."

Finishing with the buttons on her dress she shrugged it off letting it drop to the floor. Her chemise and bloomers soon followed.

He lay her down on the blanket he'd spread out on the fresh hay and came down beside her. Propping up on his forearm, he ran his fingertips up and down her stomach sending little tremors of pleasure to her core. He came back to her nipples, pinched them, bent and took one into his mouth where he teased it with his tongue. He pulled back his head and released the swollen nub with a pop and moved on to the other one. She grabbed his head in an attempt to keep him at her breast.

He chuckled and moved to her belly, kissing as he went down. Fisting the blanket in her hands, she rolled her neck while her body wound tighter and tighter with each kiss downward.

Finally he reached her slit and opened her nether lips with his fingers, baring her clit to his eager tongue. The first touch almost sent her soaring but he pulled back. "Not yet, honey. I've lots more fun to have before you come."

"No, Caleb, please. I can't take it. Please."

"Oh, darlin', you're in for a treat." With those words he entered her with one of his long fingers. "You're so tight. It feels like the first time."

"It feels to me like it's been years," she said between pants for breath. "Now finish what you started."

"Tsk. Tsk. Greedy wench, aren't you?" He put in another finger and curled the two of them until they reached her special spot. The one that made her freeze and feel everything more intensely.

"What are you doing to me?" she moaned as he scissored his fingers, tapping on the spot then putting them together to rub against it. He stopped and she settled back down. He did this time and again until she was begging for completion.

"Please. Please, Caleb. Damn you."

His fingers rubbed the spot and his mouth came down on her clit and he suckled her. As his tongue worked her, she pinched her nipples. The first wave of pleasure washed over her like the sea at the New Jersey shore. He circled her with his tongue then lapped at her like a cat with a bowl of cream.

"Caleb," she screamed and bucked against his hungry mouth.

He kept licking, shattering her, until she finally settled, out of breath and gasping. He rose over her, positioned himself between her legs and entered her slick body in one swift sure stroke. He pumped slow, his whiskey-colored eyes, black with passion, locked with hers. Bending down he took her bottom lip into his mouth and before claiming all of her mouth.

His motions became harder, more frantic. Hard, and then harder he slammed into her; sounds of flesh meeting flesh filled her ears. Then he groaned. "Maggie!" he shouted and buried his face in her neck, kissing her, sucking her, he gave her a little bite and she knew she'd have a small mark the next morning.

He rolled to his side and tucked her under his arm. "You're an amazing woman, Maggie Selby."

She cuddled into him. The breeze from the open loft door was cool against the sheen of sweat that coated her skin. "Thank you, Caleb"

"Give me some time to recover and we can do it again."

"As much as I'd like that, I have to go and finish my chores, as do you. Besides," she sat up, leaned over and kissed him. "I don't want you to get tired of me too soon."

"Maggie," he said, his eyes solemn, "I'll never get tired of you." He pulled her head down, bringing her lips back to his.

She felt his manhood stir against her belly and pulled away. "You're not taking as long as I might have thought to be prepared for round two."

"You do that to me. I'm not usually so quick to recover."

"Well, it must be later." She stood and pulled on her bloomers and chemise. Caleb watched her dress and where she'd been ashamed of her body with Edgar, preferring to make love in the dark, with Caleb, it was the opposite. He worshiped her and she suddenly felt proud and wanted to flaunt herself in front of him.

He got up and put his own clothes on.

"We have to be careful, Caleb. No one can know. Rachel wouldn't understand and everyone else would lose all respect for me."

"If you'd marry me, none of this sneaking around would be necessary," he said as he tucked his shirt into his trousers. He sat, brushed off his socks and pulled on his boots. "Turn around and let me get the hay out of your hair."

She dutifully turned her back to him and finished buttoning up her dress while he brushed his hands down her back, getting all the hay off of her that he could.

"I guess I need to bring another blanket up here for next time. We seem to roll around off the one we have. Save us both a lot of trouble cleaning up."

Smiling she said, "That would be nice." She turned in a circle in front of him. "Am I presentable?"

"You are," he kissed her nose.

"You have hay in your hair and on your shirt. Let me brush it off you."

"I'm working in the hay loft; I'm supposed to have hay on me."

She walked to the ladder and started down it. "See you at dinner. Fran's going to fix fried chicken *if* you'll kill the chickens for her."

"Yes, ma'am. How many do you want?"

"Four. The men are always especially hungry at noon meal. It's like they think they have to eat more to last until supper. They *do* know that there are always beans and stew on the stove don't they?"

"Yes. They know. They just like Fran's cooking. I'll bring the chickens up in a little while. Don't forget the milk."

"Thank you. I won't." She finished climbing down the ladder, picked up the pails of milk and walked out of the barn humming. She could definitely get used to that.

*****

Time was growing short. The weddings were today. Maggie and Rachel spent the morning after breakfast gathering wild flowers. She'd arranged them in mason jars around the parlor where the ceremony was taking place.

Caleb, Tom and Robert built a dance floor and tables for the food and drinks out in the area in front of the house. The happy couples had a band playing and planned for a lot of dancing. Half the town of Golden and all the surrounding ranchers were expected to come.

Fran and Cassie were acting as each other's maid of honor and Tom and Robert were each other's best man. Rachel was the flower girl. Cassie had even surprised her with a new blue dress with lace around the ruffle at the bottom. She looked absolutely adorable. How Cassie had managed to make three dresses in little more than two weeks, Maggie didn't know. Back in New York it took six weeks for Maggie to get three dresses. She guessed she was using the wrong modiste. A relic left over from the Edgar days. It was time to find another. Perhaps the one Cassie worked for before coming to Colorado would be a good choice considering the quality that Cassie's dresses displayed.

Maggie wore her best dress. A light green silk she'd had made in Golden for church on Sunday's. It fit her beautifully, emphasizing her small waist. She wore her hair down for the occasion, pulled back on the sides with two pearl combs. They were two of the pieces of jewelry Edgar had given her that she actually liked. Another of those pieces was an emerald broach that happened to look spectacular with her new silk dress.

The men, including Caleb, were dressed alike in three piece brown or black suits, white shirts, cravats that matched the suit and clean, black Stetson's. Each of the three men wore their Sunday suit, were handsome as the devil and each was a good man, too. Her ladies were very lucky women.

The Reverend Mr. Smith arrived to perform the ceremony. It was like one ceremony until he got to the "I do" part. Then he asked each couple separately. Once the ceremony was over both couples kissed, everyone cheered and the party started.

Caleb watched Maggie and Maria handle the

food. Fran did all the cooking the day before. All they had to do was keep the platters and bowls full. Finally it got down to the last of the chicken and Maggie felt she could enjoy the party, too.

Caleb waited patiently. He danced with each of the brides and with Rachel but no one else. He waited for Maggie.

"Are you ready to dance?" he asked when she came up to him where he stood by the hitching rail.

"I am."

"Good." He took her in his arms and they danced the waltz that was playing. The band played square dances, a Virginia Reel that was particularly popular with the crowd and several more waltzes before the night was over.

Cassie and Fran had requested they play lots of waltzes so they could dance close with their new spouses. Maggie was glad because it also meant she and Caleb could dance in each other's arms without attracting attention.

Caleb arranged for Rachel to go home with John and Sarah Atwood. They had two little girls, just a year or two older than Rachel, who was thrilled to be going to spend the night. It was lonely for her, being an only child, and these visits were a special treat.

With Cassie and Fran both out of the house, that only left Maria, who could sleep through anything. Caleb had plans for tonight that didn't include anyone but Maggie. He would finally have Maggie in his bed.

The last person finally left and Maggie started to clean up.

"Leave it," he said coming up behind her and wrapping his arms around her waist. "Come with me. Come to bed."

"I can't. You know that," she said as she leaned back against his hard chest.

He kissed the top of her head. "Rachel is staying with the Atwoods, Cassie is on her wedding night, so is Fran, and Maria won't bother us."

"You've thought of everything except the fact that I'm too tired."

"I'll make you feel better and I won't make

love to you."

She turned in his arms, looked up at him and cocked her eyebrow.

He let go of her, crossed his heart and held up his hand. "I promise. Unless of course, you ask."

She laughed and settled against his warm chest. "You never give up, do you?"

"Not where you're concerned," he said as he kissed the top of her head. He'd do anything for Maggie except give her what she most wanted. He just didn't have it in him. Didn't know how to love her the way she wanted. The way she needed. She loved him. He felt it. She couldn't respond to him the way she did without loving him. He wished he could give it back to her. If there was ever a woman he could love, it was Maggie.

CHAPTER 7

Maggie allowed Caleb to lead her to his room. She'd been in here many times over the last three months to clean but this was the first time she was in the room with him in it, too. Somehow the bed she faced from the door seemed much smaller than it did when she changed the sheets.

Caleb closed the door behind them, bringing Maggie out of her reverie. He came up behind her and again closed his arms around her waist bringing her back against his heat. "I'm going to make you feel good. Take off your clothes and lie face down in the middle of the bed."

She turned to him, a question on her lips, but

seeing his face and the loving look on it, she started unbuttoning her dress. Caleb, unable to just watch, helped her, getting her naked in record time. She was long past being embarrassed to be naked in front of him, though having him still fully clothed was a bit disconcerting. Lying face down on the bed, she asked, "Now what?"

"Now you get to relax." Strong hands began rubbing her aching shoulders and she felt cream being massaged into them. Her rose cream, by the smell of it. She felt his ministrations clear to her toes. Never in her life had she had someone simply massage her muscles. And it felt so good. She hadn't realized how sore she was until now when he smoothed his hands over and over her, applying pressure and soothing her aching body at the same time.

"How's this feel?"

"Wonderful. I might go to sleep."

"If that's what you need, then do it. I'll be right here. I'm not going anywhere, Maggie."

She got the feeling that he meant that in more

ways than just staying with her tonight but she was too tired to question it very hard.

Warmth. She was cuddled into Caleb's side and was incredibly warm. Too warm. She threw off the blankets and rolled away from him. Her body still languid from the wonderful massage he'd given her, she fell back asleep.

Later, she woke again. Her throat was dry. She was so thirsty but weak. "Caleb. Caleb."

"What?" he mumbled, his voice heavy with sleep.

"I don't feel good. I need water."

He sat up and lit the lamp at the bedside.

"Maggie?" concern laced his voice. He reached over and put his hand on her forehead. "You're burning up."

She nodded. "So hot."

He got up and got a glass of water from the pitcher on the commode and took it to her. She was so weak she couldn't hold the glass and so he held it for her while she sipped. After she'd gotten her fill, he put water into the basin next to the pitcher and wrung out a soft washcloth in the cool water.

He came back to the bed and laid it on her forehead. She turned into the coolness.

"Ah, Maggie, you're sick. You worked too hard on this wedding."

She moaned.

"I'm going to go make you some tea. You get some rest and I'll be right back."

She tried to nod her head but the pain shot through it and all she could do was close her eyes tight and press the cloth more firmly against her forehead.

Caleb pulled on his pants and went to the kitchen. She was asleep when he got back. He hoped she slept while he was gone, but now he needed to get the tea in her.

"Here, sweetheart, drink this."

He helped her to sit up some and then held a cup of hot tea for her to sip at. He'd put honey in it so it would soothe her throat.

"Not too fast. It's hot."

She lay back down and tried to shove the

covers off of herself. "So hot."

"You've got a fever. I'll get you some willow bark tea and it will help to break the fever and with your headache."

"Thank you."

He pulled the covers up around her chin. "I'll be back. Stay under the covers."

As soon as he was out of the room she must have kicked off the covers and got up, went to the window and opened it. When Caleb returned she was sitting on the floor under the window.

"Damn it, Maggie. What do you think you're doing? You'll take a chill." He set the tea on the night table, then went and picked her up in his arms.

"It was too hot," she murmured.

He put her back in bed and pulled the covers up around her chest, leaving her arms bare. Then he helped her drink the willow bark tea. It was still the middle of the night and he knew it was going to be a long one.

After he got her settled he left again and came back with one of her nightgowns. Then he took the washcloth she'd abandoned in the bed, rewet it and began to stroke it down her arms and across her chest.

She relaxed under his caring hands and fell asleep.

Maggie was too hot. He worked to keep her cool and to break the fever that had her gripped in its claws. He stroked the cool cloth up and down her arms, back and forth across her chest. By the time he'd gotten one pass, the cloth was already warm from her fevered skin. He rewet it in the cool water and started again.

After he'd cooled her down a bit, he had her drink some more of the willow bark tea until it was all gone. He'd make some more in a couple of hours if her fever still hadn't broken. She'd fallen asleep again and seemed to be resting peacefully. He lay down beside her gathered her into his arms and fell asleep.

Something hit him in the chest waking him instantly. Maggie was thrashing, deep in the throes of some nightmare no doubt brought on by her fever.

"Shh. Maggie. Sweetheart. Wake up," he said gently while he gathered her into his arms again.

She struggled for an instant and then settled against him. Her fever still raged. He'd have to wake Maria. He needed help to get it down.

Getting up from the bed, he pulled on a shirt and went to get Maria.

They returned with a fresh pitcher of water and another basin. Caleb moved a chair next to the bed for her.

"Maria, I'd appreciate it if you…,"

She shook her head. "Mr. Caleb, I won't say anything. What you and Mrs. Maggie do is your business. Let's just get her well."

He nodded. "Thank you."

They worked the rest of the night bathing Maggie in cool water. About daybreak, her fever finally broke and she awakened.

"Caleb?"

"Yes, sweetheart. I'm here."

"Thirsty."

"Okay. Here you go." He held the glass to her lips and let her drink her fill. Then he put it back on the night stand.

Maria was still there and got up to leave.

"Thank you , for your help, Maria," said Caleb

"You're welcome. I'll leave you now. I must fix breakfast while Fran is gone,

"I'll be down in a bit. Do you think you could fix some broth for her?"

"Of course. I'll start the bones to boiling. It won't be ready for several hours. Maybe a biscuit or some cornmeal mush for now?"

"Maggie, what would you like?"

"Nothing."

"You need to eat something," said Caleb.

"A biscuit, then."

Maria turned to Caleb, "You come to the kitchen in a twenty minutes and it will be ready."

After Maria left, Maggie tried to get up.

"What are you doing?" asked Caleb holding her down with a hand on her chest.

"Need to go to the bathroom," she said pushing

at his hand.

He let her up. "Let me help you."

She stood on her own beside the bed, but didn't move.

"Here," he put his arm around her waist. "Lean on me." He took her behind the screen where the chamber pot was. The screen was Ruth's idea, one he'd liked and kept.

When she was ready, he helped her back to the bed.

"I can't stay here," she said when he tried to put her back in bed.

"Why not?"

"Rachel will be home soon. I can't be in your bed."

"Alright, I'll take you back to your room. I got you a nightgown."

"Thank you. For everything."

"You're welcome." He helped her put on the gown and then picked her up in his arms and started walking to her room.

"Put me down."

"No. I don't want you falling. Whatever it was that made you sick also made you weak."

"It must have, because I don't have the energy to fight with you."

He smiled. "Then now would be a good time for me to ask you again to marry me."

"I lost my energy, not my mind."

He got her tucked into bed and then left for the kitchen to check on her breakfast.

*****

When Caleb got to the kitchen, Maria wasn't there but was outside cussing someone. He went out of the house to see what the furor was about. Martin Butler and Maria were yelling at one another. Maria stood on the porch off the kitchen and Butler was at the bottom of the steps.

"Butler, I warned you. Get off my property."

"Hold your horses, Black. I didn't come to see Mrs. Selby."

"Then what are you doing here?"

"I still need a wife. You got moren' yer fair share of women. I came to court the ornery one yelling at me."

"You came to court me? What makes you think I'd want anything to do with an old fart like you?"

"You're not no spring chicken, ya old hen."

"Doesn't sound to me like she wants to be courted by you," said Caleb.

Maria turned to face him where he stood on the porch. "Now, Mr. Caleb, let's not be hasty here."

Caleb raised his eyebrows but nodded. "Go on, Butler. The lady seems to want to hear what you have to say after all."

"I just came to ask if she'd like to go with me to the church social on Saturday."

Maria put her hands on her hips. "Well then ask *me* you old fool, not Mr. Caleb."

"Well do ya?"

She thought about it a bit. "Yes. Bring a buggy." With that, she turned and walked back in the house.

Butler looked up at Caleb. "I'll be back on Saturday." He turned, went to his horse, mounted and galloped down the drive.

Well I'll be, thought Caleb. *Maggie was right.*

He picked up her biscuit and another cup of tea and then headed back to tell Maggie the latest happenings.

"You'll never guess who was in our yard at this ungodly hour."

"You're right. I won't guess." She took a sip of tea and then closed her eyes and leaned back against the pillows.

"Martin Butler."

Maggie's eyes popped open. "What!? You didn't say anything to him about me. Oh Caleb, don't tell me you shot him."

Caleb sat on the side of the bed and began stroking her hair. "No. I didn't shoot him."

She relaxed. "So what did you do? What did he bring me this time?"

"Not a thing."

"Nothing?" asked Maggie.

"Nope. He did have some flowers with him but they weren't for you."

"Then who? Oh," she said suddenly realizing. "Maria."

Caleb nodded. "They're going to the church social on Saturday. Oh, I sent one of my cowboys to John and Sarah's asking if they'd keep Rachel for another few days. I'm sure they won't mind. I'd rather have you well when she comes home. And just in case this is contagious I don't want her catching it."

Maggie sat up in bed. "That's good. I don't want her to get sick either. What about you and Maria? You could get sick."

"Calm down. We're fine and we intend to stay that way. I think this was brought on by exhaustion. You worked too hard preparing for the weddings. All you need is a couple of days rest and you'll be right as rain."

"I hope you're right. I feel like I've been rode hard and put away wet, as your cowboys would say. I'm so tired."

"Rest now. I'll be back in a few hours to check on you. Will you be alright until then?"

"Yes. You go. I know you have chores to do."

He nodded. Dropped a kiss on her forehead and left.

*****

By the end of the third day, Maggie was going stir crazy. Caleb brought her every meal and ate with her. He came and sat with her every evening and then lay with her until she fell asleep. She was fine now. Determined to get up and back to her work, she got out of bed and dressed in her blue cotton dress. The one he'd remembered chafed her neck. She'd tucked a scarf around her collar so it wouldn't hurt her today. She smiled at the memory and still couldn't believe that he'd remembered something so trivial. She was a little wobbly but felt that was because she'd been in bed for three days.

She went down to the kitchen to help Maria. Fran wasn't supposed to be back for another couple of days. She and Tom went on a little trip to Denver, stayed for a few days, and then took another few days to work on the cabin. Tom wanted it to be nice for Fran and she wanted to make curtains and clean it really well before she moved in.

They wouldn't have the room for Maria finished for another month or so which wasn't a bad thing. The newlyweds needed some time alone together.

Without Fran to do the cooking it was left to Maria. She was up to the task but Maggie thought she could probably use some help anyway.

"Maria, what can I do to help you?"

"Mrs. Maggie, what are you doing out of bed? Mr. Caleb will have my hide if he sees you here."

"I was going crazy in that room. I need to get out and get some fresh air."

"Then you go outside and sit on the porch. Don't do anything but rest. You were very sick; you must get your strength back."

Maggie sat at the table with a cup of coffee from the big pot on the stove. There was always coffee and always a stew or beans warm on the stove for whenever the men needed something to eat.

"How am I going to get my strength back if I just lie about in bed? I need to be working, moving. At the very least I should help you with the food."

"No. I've heard about your cooking. It would be best if you left the food to me."

Maggie knew she blushed. Her one and only meal had gone over well. Everyone ate it and seemed to want more. But maybe they were just being polite. She didn't think she was a bad cook, but she hadn't showed what she could really do either. And it had been a long time since she'd cooked for more than one person.

"Then I need to do Rachel's chores, gathering the eggs and milking the cows. She's not home yet, so I can do that."

Maria rolled her eyes and shook her head. "You are a stubborn woman, Mrs. Maggie."

"You don't know the half of it." Caleb's deep baritone voice washed over her from the open doorway. "Why aren't you in bed?"

"I'm tired and bored and I want to do

something. I'm going to go gather the eggs and milk the cows."

"No you're not. I'll do it if Maria can't."

"She's too busy preparing breakfast for the men. Dang it, Caleb. I can do this." She almost never cussed but she was so frustrated she couldn't help it.

"Tsk. Tsk. I'll have to wash out your mouth with soap."

She pouted. "Please Caleb. I'm going crazy. I need to be up and doing. I won't over do it and if I need to, I'll stop and take a rest or a nap."

"I'll come with you." When she would have protested, he said, "just to make sure you don't fall over from exhaustion. We saw how well that went last time."

She picked up the egg basket. "Alright, let's go."

The chicken coop wasn't far and she had no problem getting the eggs. She didn't do it often, it was after all Rachel's job, but she remembered to go behind the hens to take their egg. Caleb had three dozen laying hens and another dozen he kept for eating. They bought chickens every month to replenish the eating chickens.

Caleb walked with her back to the house. She was feeling a little tired from just that little bit of work but knew she needed to do it to get back her stamina.

"How are you feeling?"

"I'm fine. A little walk to and from the chicken coop isn't going to kill me."

He chuckled. "Fiery as ever. I didn't say it would kill you, just thought you might be a little tired."

"Nope. I'm good," she lied. "Let me get the milk pails and you can walk with me to the barn." She pasted on a happy smile and picked up the milk buckets. "Here," she handed him the pails. "Make yourself useful."

They walked to the barn. A fair distance from the house. So much so that by the time they got there, Maggie was glad for the stool to sit on. Caleb rubbed her neck and back as usual though the milking itself wasn't tiring. At least she didn't think so until she stood up. She groaned upon rising, every muscle aching.

"I feel like I was in a stampede and every cow stomped me. I hate to admit it but you may have been right. Doing the milking was more than I should have tried for my first day.

Caleb picked up both milk pails. "I'm not going to say 'I told you so' but you need to ease your way back in to your regular routine."

They walked in silence for a little while.

"Tell me something. Would you be treating Fran or Maria like this?

"I would definitely be concerned, but no, I wouldn't be treating them the way I do you. Though I like them well enough, I don't care for them like I do you."

There it was. That word again. *Care*. If he told her one more time he *cared* for her, she'd scream. But it was one more reason for her to leave. He was never going to love her. Really love her, like she did him. With every essence of her being. With all her heart and soul.

*****

The bout with the illness and fever sapped her strength and put her behind. She slowly built it back up until she felt well enough to travel. It was time.

At supper that night, she told Caleb, "I need to talk to you after supper."

"Alright. In the parlor, as usual."

"I just wanted to make sure you'd be there."

"I will."

She nodded.

After supper she arrived in the parlor before he did. She couldn't settle, her nerves on edge. She paced back and forth in front of the fire so deep in her thoughts she didn't hear him come in.

"Something's bothering you. Spit it out."

She jumped at his voice. After she took a deep breath, she said, "It's time. I'm going back to New York. I'd like someone to take me into Denver tomorrow so I can catch the train the following day."

He was silent it seemed like forever. "I knew it was coming but I hoped to change your mind. We're made to be together, Maggie. You know it was well as I do."

Her hands shook; she fisted them at her sides. "I can't give up everything for a marriage without love. I've had one like that and I won't do it again. Being good at sex doesn't mean we're good together. I need more."

"I wish I could give it to you." He turned toward the fire. "I really do. I've given you all I have to give."

Tears filled her eyes but she refused to let them fall. She didn't know why she expected something different, but she had. After all the time they'd spent together, she hoped he'd see that he loved her, but it was to no avail.

"So, will you have someone take me to Denver?"

"I'll ask Tom."

"Thank you. I'll go pack now. Please tell Rachel goodbye for me."

"I will. She's going to miss you."

He turned back to face her. She saw the anguish on his face and wanted to run into his arms and tell him it was all a mistake. That it would be alright. But she couldn't. This was real.

"And I her."

"This is going to break her heart."

"Do you think this is what I want? Do you really think I want to leave the two people I love most in the world? It's killing me but better quickly now than slowly if I stay."

CHAPTER 8

September 23, 1871

Maggie arrived back in New York without much trouble. She'd had a stomach problem that left her sick in the mornings but she always felt better by the afternoon and was able to eat. Having made the trip once, she knew where to get food and where to avoid. All in all, the trip was pleasant enough, if she hadn't been running away from everything she wanted. Was having him tell her he loved her really that important? Didn't he show it in other ways? He did love her, she was sure of it, but he needed to be sure of it, too.

Marriage scared her to death. Edgar had seen to that. Seen to it that every girlish notion she had about love and marriage was destroyed by the reality of her marriage to him. Though in her heart, she knew Caleb wasn't Edgar, but without that declaration of love from him, she couldn't give herself over completely. She needed it like she needed air to breathe and water to drink. She needed his love for her very survival.

The cab pulled up in front of her three story building. She saw the office curtains were open and probably should check in with Sally, but tomorrow would be soon enough. Too tired to do much of anything except get her valises up the stairs and fall into bed, she went to the door leading to the apartments above the office.

She walked into her apartment and immediately felt the walls close in. It was stuffy and small and with all the windows closed it was hot. She opened the windows and attempted to get a breeze flowing through but only felt the heat. New York was having a late summer. The heat rose off the streets and into her little apartment. She missed the wide open spaces of the Colorado Territory, where if you wanted, you could go days without seeing another person. She missed Caleb's house with its big rooms and the pretty picture window in the parlor. She missed Rachel. But most of all she missed Caleb.

He was constantly in her thoughts, especially since she figured out that the impossible had happened. Her sickness on the train wasn't left over from the fever she'd had, but was morning sickness. She was pregnant with Caleb's baby. A miracle to be sure, but what was she going to tell Caleb. Should she tell him at all? They were thousands of miles apart and would likely not see each other again, but he deserved to know. Just thinking about it gave her a headache.

Able to lie down for the first time in seven days, she collapsed on the bed for a nap. When she woke it was dark outside. She lit the lamp she kept on the bedside table and glanced at the clock next to it. It was just past midnight. She'd slept for more than nine hours and now she was starving. There was nothing in the house to eat, but she still had an apple and some bread from the train trip. Of course, she always had tea and she put a pot on to boil. She'd visit the market tomorrow and stock up on food.

She'd been gone for nearly five months. It was a good thing she'd planned ahead. Knowing she'd be gone for a minimum of three weeks, she'd stopped her milk delivery and cleaned out her ice box before she left.

Sitting at her little dining table she drank the fragrant tea and wished it was the strong, bitter coffee from Caleb's stove. She wished she knew what to do. Here she was, thirty-five years old, pregnant and alone.

She estimated the baby would be due in about seven months but would get her doctor to confirm. Actually, she'd find a new doctor to confirm. Her current doctor, because she saw him so rarely, was also a remnant of her past that she needed to get rid of.

It probably happened during the time they spent at the line shack. Maybe even the first time. Two glorious days where they pretended that no one else existed. They couldn't get enough of each other. It was a wonderful two days. The most wonderful of her life.

Her eyes filled with tears and she let them flow. There was so reason not to. No one to see or care if she cried or not.

*****

Maggie threw herself into her work. She made more matches than ever before. Good matches. It was like she was possessed.

She found a new doctor, a woman doctor, Dr. Martha Berringer. As to her pregnancy, Dr. Berringer agreed that she was due in seven months, based on the timing of her menses and the look of her cervix. Seven months. So much could happen in seven months.

One hundred dollars. That was the amount that she owed Caleb. She sent it to him as soon as she could, taking her savings account down to almost in

214

half. It'd taken her five years to save that much money and now she had to start over. Another reason to work harder. She had a baby to provide for now and needed to have that savings built up for when the little one came and she couldn't work for a while. Although, since she owned her own business, it was completely probable the baby would come to work with her. After all, she made her own rules. Who was going to naysay her anyway?

The months passed in a blur filled with work and doctor appointments. The doctor worried about her because this was her first pregnancy and she was very old for having a baby. Soon it was only a month until the baby was due.

One late March day, Maggie was sitting at her desk doing the final paperwork for her latest match when the bell above the door sounded. She glanced up and was shocked to see Cassie in the doorway.

"Maggie!" said Cassie as she ran to her.

Maggie rose as quickly as her bulk would let her. "Cassie. How are you? What are you doing in

New York? Where is Robert?"

Cassie laughed. "Robert is still at the hotel seeing about the luggage. I couldn't wait and took a cab to see you. He'll be along shortly." She looked Maggie up and down. "I guess you have some news to share. The same kind of news that Robert and I have."

"Oh, my, that's wonderful. When are you expecting the sweet thing to show its face to the world?"

"In about five months. But from the looks of you, yours will be here much, much sooner than that."

Maggie automatically put her hand on her belly. "He'll be here in about a month, give or take a week or two."

"Were you going to tell Caleb?"

"I was, then I wasn't, then I was. Oh, Cassie, I haven't known what to do and now, well, it's probably best he doesn't know. He doesn't love me and I won't marry or raise a child with someone who doesn't love me."

"Come sit down before you fall over. I have to tell you, you're huge. I don't mean that in a bad way, just an observation. I've never seen anyone carry their baby so...heavy."

Maggie sat down behind her desk again. "I know. The doctor thought I might be carrying twins, but can only find evidence of one baby. I would have asked my mother if she carried us so heavy but I don't want my parents to know. Ever. I'll never let my father get his filthy paws on my son."

"You keep saying son and he. Do you really believe you're having a boy?"

She smiled and rubbed her belly. "I do. I had a dream that I had a little boy in Caleb's spitting image and since then I've been calling him a boy."

"So what are you going to do about Caleb?"

"I don't know. He doesn't love me. He said he *cares* for me but he'll never love me. Not like I deserve." She shook her head, resigned. "I can't live in another loveless marriage."

Cassie cocked her head and rolled her eyes in

obvious disbelief. "Doesn't love you? Are you an idiot? He's crazy for you and since you've been gone he's just been crazy. He's a bear and hardly anyone can stand to be around him. We do, mostly for Rachel's sake. She misses you something fierce and so does her daddy."

Maggie shook her head. "He said he'd never—"

"Because he doesn't know what it is. It's hard to say you can love someone unless you've experienced love to begin with. He hadn't. Not until you."

She looked across the desk at the younger woman. "You've matured so well. Marriage seems to agree with you."

The bell above the door sounded again and Robert walked in, a big smile on his face when he looked at his wife. Then he looked at Maggie and his face fell.

"Shit. Caleb's going to be pissed you didn't tell him, Maggie. What were you thinking?"

Maggie started to rise and Robert rushed to her

side to help her.

She waved him off. "I've been getting up and down on my own just fine, Robert, though I thank you for the thoughtfulness. As to Caleb. I don't know what I've been thinking. It's changes on a daily basis. Right now, I think it's none of his business."

"None of his business?? You can't be serious. Do you expect us to believe that the father is someone other than Caleb?" asked Robert.

Tears filled her eyes. She was extremely moody and cried at the drop of a hat. The doctor assured her that was normal.

"Don't yell at me, Robert. You think I haven't gone over every scenario in my head? Do you think I really want to raise my child without a father?"

"Maggie," said Cassie, "now is not the time to be stubborn. Your baby deserves to know he has a wonderful father, who loves him very much."

She sniffled and then dabbed at her eyes with the hanky she kept up her sleeve for such a purpose. "He would love the baby, wouldn't he? Even if he only cares for me. I'm just so confused right now. Every time I start to write to him, I stop because I don't know what to say."

Robert looked at Cassie with furrowed brow. "What is she talking about?"

"She believes that Caleb doesn't love her."

"What? That's nonsense. He's been the most unhappy man I've ever seen. I didn't see him this broken up after Ruth died."

"You both think I've made a huge mistake don't you?"

"I'm afraid you have," said Cassie gently. "You never needed to go through this by yourself. You should wire Caleb."

"I can't. Not now. Not after all this time. What if he doesn't want me? Or us? What if...?" She started bawling. All the tears she'd refused to shed now flowed from her, unchecked.

Cassie patted Maggie's back. "Alright. Calm down. You won't wire him. What are you going to do then?"

"I'm going to continue with my plans. I'm

going to have this baby and raise him the best I can." She hiccupped. "I've been doing extra work and have my nest egg built up so I can take some time off when he comes. I know a western woman would probably have the baby and keep right on working but I'm not a western woman."

"What makes you think that?" Robert asked.

"I'm just assuming they are much stronger than I am."

Robert came around the desk. "Maggie, you are one of the strongest women I've ever met. Also one of the most stubborn and idiotic. Wire Caleb. Let him know he's going to be a father again. I guarantee he'll be thrilled."

She shook her head. "I can't."

"Okay, we won't push you. And I don't want you crying anymore," said Cassie. "How about we go out to dinner and catch up on all the gossip from Golden? I've been dying to share it with someone."

Maggie laughed. "I'd love to hear it and about everyone back at the ranch."

"Good. We need to freshen up after the train

ride but we'll be back about six and we'll take Robert for some Italian food. He's never had it before."

"Oh, you're in for a treat, Robert."

"So, I've been told."

Maggie shooed them out the door and went upstairs to freshen herself up.

Once outside, Cassie turned to Robert. "I don't care what Maggie thinks she wants, Caleb needs to know. Let's go to the Western Union office and send him a wire. He can be on tomorrow's train."

"Agreed. It's not going to be pretty when he gets here. He'll have had a week to stew over it."

"Then he needs to come see us first. I want to explain to him why Maggie made the decision she did. Maybe he'll understand and realize that part of the blame falls on his shoulders," said Cassie.

"I doubt he'll understand. Men like Caleb really *don't* know what love is, so caring is as close as he can come. Let's go get this done so I can take my beautiful bride back to the room and make love to her before we have to leave for dinner."

Cassie turned and smiled up at him. "Yes, sir. Anything you want."

*****

Pregnant. She was pregnant. Why didn't she tell him? Didn't she know he'd take care of her? Marry her. Give the baby a name. It was his child. His son or daughter. He had a right to know. Why wouldn't she tell him? They'd shared so much. Why would she keep this a secret? These questions went over and over in Caleb's mind the entire trip from Denver to New York and he still had no answers. She knew he cared for her. Hell, he'd never cared so much for anyone as he did Maggie.

The train arrived at the station three hours late. They'd hit a wagon carrying steel pipe and getting the tracks cleared and checking the train to make sure it was on the tracks properly after the accident had taken time. Robert and Cassie were supposed to meet him but with the train's delay had not stayed, which he could understand. They'd given him explicit instructions to go see them before seeing Maggie, but he couldn't wait. He had

Maggie's address from their correspondence all those months ago. It seemed like years now with all that had happened.

He hailed a cab and gave the driver Maggie's address. What would he say to her now? He had to remember to keep his temper. She had her reasons, though he couldn't imagine what would make her keep this a secret. She knew how he felt about kids. He wanted lots of them and Rachel wanted brothers and sisters. She mentioned it often. Or at least she had before Maggie left. Now she didn't mention it at all. Or wanting a mother either.

He'd been wrong to let her become so close to Maggie who'd made it clear she didn't intend to stay. Maggie warned him. He'd just been too stubborn to believe it. Always thought he could change her mind. He'd been wrong.

The cab pulled up in front of Maggie's building. It was almost 4 pm and he didn't know if she'd still be open but he knew she lived on the second floor so he'd go there if he had to. She was not going to put him off.

He went to the door and saw the little open sign. Would it be Maggie inside or Sally, her assistant? His hands were clammy and he wiped them on his pants before he turned the knob.

The bell over the door sounded.

"I'll be with you in just a minute" said the red haired woman with her back to him. He'd recognize that voice anywhere. She was standing on a ladder with a stack of files on her arm. She was filing and standing on a ladder...Caleb thought he might hyperventilate, he was so scared she'd fall. He didn't say a word but went over to stand at the bottom of the ladder.

"What do you think you're doing?"

Maggie squealed and lost her footing. Files went everywhere as she landed safely in Caleb's arms.

"What are you doing here? Put me down."

"I don't think so. You'll just do something stupid like climb back up on that ladder. Does Sally know you do that?" When she was silent, he said, "I thought so."

She'd stiffened in his arms. It was like trying to hold a sack of stone. He carried her safely away from the shelves to her desk and sat down with her in his arms.

"I said put me down."

"You're down. As down as you're going to get."

She looked up at him, her green eyes full of unshed tears.

"Ah, hell. Don't do that, Maggie. There's no reason to cry."

She sniffled and fat tears rolled down her cheeks. "There's every reason to cry. You're here because Cassie told you. Don't deny it. She wired you, must have been that first day for you to be here now. Why did you bother to come?"

"Because you're pregnant. Why didn't you tell me? I'd have taken care of you."

"That's just the point. I don't want to be *taken care of*. My baby doesn't want to be *taken care of*. Well, he does and I will, but…oh, you know what I mean."

"I came because I couldn't stay away."

"You mean because I'm pregnant. Because you haven't had any problems staying away until now."

"No, not because you're pregnant. That's a bonus. I mean I couldn't stay away any longer because of you. It's been killing me. Every time I go to the barn, I expect to see you milking the cows or I see you in the hay loft with your glorious hair cascading around you after we made love. I can't go to the line shack without thinking of you. Of us."

"What are you saying to me, Caleb? Say it straight out because I don't want there to be any misunderstandings."

He kissed her and to his surprise she let him, didn't pull away. "Maggie, I care for you more than I ever have anyone. I don't know if that's love but I think it could be. I think I love you, Maggie. I know I want to be with you. I want to raise our child...children together. I miss your smile and your laugh. I miss you being mad at me and poking me in the arm when you think I'm wrong. I miss everything about you. I want to wake up beside you for the rest of our lives. I want you to drive me crazy with your matchmaking. I want to be with you. Forever. I don't want to have to go another day without you."

She sobbed. With every word he said she sobbed harder. It was the sweetest, most wonderful declaration of love she'd ever had. He may not have said it outright but he loved her. It was there for the entire world to see in the way he treated her, the way he listened when she talked. In every letter he'd sent her. In the way he laughed at her jokes.

The baby decided it was time for him to be heard from. He kicked her hard. Hard enough that Caleb felt it, his hand covering her belly.

He looked up at her, "He wants you to say you'll marry me Maggie. Not just because we're good together, which we are, but because we love each other and for me at least, there is no one else. Never will be."

She cried and laughed. "You really mean that

don't you?"

"Of course. I wouldn't say it if I didn't mean it. It's too important to me, to us. I love you, Maggie and I want you to be my wife and the mother to our children."

She took his beloved face in her hands and kissed him. "I love you, Caleb Black and I will marry you."

"When? I want it to be right away. I want to be married when the baby is born."

"That could be any time now. The doctor says I've got another few weeks but I think her calculation is wrong. I think I got pregnant the first time we made love."

"The first time. Wow. We're fertile."

"Apparently. It was Edgar who couldn't have children. All these years I've blamed myself because he did and now I find out he was wrong. It explains why none of his mistresses had children."

"To hell with Edgar. I don't want to hear the bastard's name ever again. The only thing I'm grateful to him for is dying. If he hadn't, you wouldn't have started your business and I'd never have met you."

She smiled and cuddled into his chest...content. "I'm so happy. Let's go tell Cassie and Robert. They can stand up with us while they're still here."

They went to the hotel where Cassie and Robert were staying. Robert answered the door when Caleb knocked.

"Well, you two are together, I guess that bodes well. Cassie, look what the cat dragged in," Robert called to Cassie.

Cassie squealed. "Oh, Maggie, I just knew you and Caleb would work it out and being that you're here together I can only assume you did. I'm so happy for you."

Cassie and Maggie hugged each other as much as Maggie's baby belly would let them.

"Congratulations," said Robert extending his hand to Caleb.

"Thanks. It's about time." Caleb shook his hand. "I can't believe it took me this long to realize

I love her."

"I can't believe it either. Everyone else knew. You've been a bear to live with since she left."

Maggie listened with one ear to Cassie and one to the conversation between Caleb and Robert. It make her happy to hear Caleb declare his love for her.

"Let's go celebrate. You two aren't the only ones with something to celebrate. Robert and I are expecting our first baby. That's why we came to New York. We won't be able to do it after the baby comes so it was now or never."

"I know and it's such wonderful news. Now our little one will have a playmate, well at least when we see you. I wish you lived closer," Maggie hugged Cassie again then they both sat on the sofa in the room.

Robert and Cassie had a small suite. Robert must have paid a fortune to get it. It had a bed, dresser and night stands as well as a sofa, two arm chairs and small table and two dining chairs. It also had a private bath. It was almost as big as Maggie's apartment.

The men sat in the arm chairs facing Maggie and Cassie.

"So are we going to Luigi's?" asked Maggie. "The boys haven't ever had food like Luigi makes. He makes the best Italian food in New York. You're going to love it."

"Yes. Let's go now and we can beat the rush for dinner," said Cassie. "I've been craving spaghetti for weeks now."

"Me, too. When we get back home we'll have to ask Fran if she knows how to make it. She is Italian after all. Or maybe Maria brought a recipe with her from Italy."

"Okay, Caleb, I need help getting up off this sofa. It's sort of swallowed me."

He took her hands and pulled her up from where she'd sunk down into the soft cushions of the divan.

"It's not easy getting around with this baby. He's getting bigger and bigger every day and so am I."

"Maybe I should carry you everywhere," said Caleb scooping her up in his arms.

"Oh," laughed Maggie. "Put me down. I'm too heavy for you."

"You're light as a feather." As if to prove it he spun her around in a circle.

"Alright you two. Quit fooling around and let's go eat," said Robert, taking Cassie's arm.

Caleb put Maggie down and the four of them left for dinner.

*****

Later that night Maggie and Caleb laid in bed, wrapped in each other's arms after making love. Their coupling had been frenzied, each of them unable to get enough of the other or to touch each other fast enough.

She had her head on his chest and was playing with the light sprinkling of soft hair on his chest. "I want to be home when the baby is born."

"Do we have enough time? I don't want it to be born on the train."

"If we leave right away we will. I don't think

he'll come for another two weeks or so."

"What about your business? How are you going to pack everything up that quickly?"

"I'm not. Sally's going to keep this office open. I'll open one in Golden after the baby gets a little older and, in the mean time, I'll work out of your office. It'll work like it did before I left."

He didn't say anything for a while just rubbed his hand up and down her arm. Then he tightened his hold on her. "I'm sorry you had to leave to get me to realize I love you. I've never been as miserable in my life as I have been these last six months."

"I needed to know that you knew you loved me. It wasn't enough for me to love you, I had to know you loved me back."

"I understand that now. Let me show you how much I love you."

"Yes, please. I've missed you, missed us."

They made slow, sweet love this time.

*****

"Caleb!"

He came running from the parlor where the doctor had sent him to wait. When he heard her yell, there was no way he was waiting to see her. Bursting into the room, he saw the doctor at her feet, her legs bent at the knee and spread wide.

"Well, don't just stand there, son. If you're going to be in here make yourself useful and hold her hand. Maggie, you squeeze his hand hard as you need to when you feel a contraction. We're almost there. Ready?"

"Yes, Doc," she panted. "Ohhh, God, Caleb."

"I'm here, sweetheart. Squeeze my hand."

"Breathe and give me a good push, now," said the doctor. "Push, Maggie, push hard."

She beared down, squeezing Caleb's hand until she couldn't any longer. Then she lay back and panted trying to get her breath.

"Rest a minute, then when I say, you give me one more push. Okay. We've almost got us a baby here. Now. Push!"

She pushed and with a whoosh, the baby slid out into the doctor's waiting hands. "Well, now it looks like we have a little boy." He tied off the cord and clipped it then handed the baby to Maria, who was helping him. She took the baby to the commode where there was a basin of warm water and cleaned him up. Then she bundled him up and handed him to Caleb.

"Here you go, Papa. Say hello to your new son,"

Caleb took the baby and sat down on the bed with him. He unwrapped him and gave him to Maggie. She counted all his fingers and toes, ran her fingers through his dark brown hair. Just like in her dream, the baby was the spitting image of Caleb. Except for his eyes. He had Maggie's clear green eyes.

"What shall we name him?" she asked.

"What would you like to name him? We could name him after our fathers."

"I'm not naming my son Ezra. I couldn't saddle the poor little thing with a name like that. Besides, my father is a bastard and I wouldn't name a child of mine after him anyway."

"Then let's call him Lawrence. I always liked that name. I had a friend as a boy who was named Lawrence. We called him Larry."

"Larry Black. I like it."

The baby started to fuss and she opened her nightgown and put him to her breast. He nuzzled her and looked for her nipple. She helped him to find it and he started to suckle.

"Isn't he beautiful?" She looked up at her husband. "He's beautiful just like his papa and his big sister. You should go get her. She needs to meet her new brother."

Caleb smiled, "Be right back."

A few minutes later he and Rachel returned.

She came up to the bed and peeked at the baby still nursing.

"Well, what do you think?" Maggie asked Rachel.

"He's awful little," said Rachel, her voice full of awe.

"He'll grow fast," said Caleb. "Before you know it, he'll be running after you and getting into everything and driving you crazy."

"Nah," said Rachel, taking little Larry's fingers in her hand, "He's gonna be my best friend."

ABOUT THE AUTHOR

Cynthia Woolf is the award winning and best-selling author of nineteen historical western romance books and two short stories with more books on the way. She was born in Denver, Colorado and raised in the mountains west of Golden. She spent her early years running wild around the mountain side with her friends.

Their closest neighbor was about one quarter of a mile away, so her little brother was her playmate and her best friend. That fierce friendship lasted until his death in 2006.

Cynthia loves writing and reading romance. Her first western romance Tame A Wild Heart, was inspired by the story her mother told her of meeting Cynthia's father on a ranch in Creede, Colorado. Although Tame A Wild Heart takes place in Creede that is the only similarity between the stories. Her father was a cowboy not a bounty hunter and her mother was a nursemaid (called a nanny now) not the ranch owner.

Cynthia credits her wonderfully supportive husband Jim and the great friends she's made at CRW for saving her sanity and allowing her to explore her creativity.

TITLES AVAILABLE

THORPE'S MAIL-ORDER BRIDE, Montana Sky

Series (Kindle Worlds)

GENEVIEVE: Bride of Nevada, American Mail-Order Brides Series

THE HUNTER BRIDE – Hope's Crossing, Book 1

THE REPLACEMENT BRIDE – Hope's Crossing, Book 2

GIDEON – The Surprise Brides

MAIL ORDER OUTLAW – The Brides of Tombstone, Book 1

MAIL ORDER DOCTOR – The Brides of Tombstone, Book 2

MAIL ORDER BARON – The Brides of Tombstone, Book 3

NELLIE – The Brides of San Francisco 1

ANNIE – The Brides of San Francisco 2

CORA – The Brides of San Francisco 3

JAKE (Book 1, Destiny in Deadwood series)

LIAM (Book 2, Destiny in Deadwood series)

ZACH (Book 3, Destiny in Deadwood series)

CAPITAL BRIDE (Book 1, Matchmaker & Co. series)

HEIRESS BRIDE (Book 2, Matchmaker & Co. series)

FIERY BRIDE (Book 3, Matchmaker & Co. series)

TAME A WILD HEART (Book 1, Tame series)

TAME A WILD WIND (Book 2, Tame series)

TAME A WILD BRIDE (Book 3, Tame series)

TAME A SUMMER HEART (short story, Tame series)

TAME A HONEYMOON HEART (novella, Tame series)

WEBSITE – http://cynthiawoolf.com/

NEWSLETTER - http://bit.ly/1qBWhFQ